# BOOK GiRL

### and the Scribe Who Faced God Part 2
### Mizuki Nomura

"Don't forget that, please.
You are Tohko's author."
RYUTO SAKURAI

"Could I . . .
have that scarf?"
NANASE KOTOBUKI

"You could never
be an author."
KANAKO SAKURAI

"Why did you turn it
down?! Why did you
throw it away?!"
TOHKO AMANO

"I always thought if I could meet a woman like that, I'd be set."

"I love it. I'll take good care of it."

"It's club time, Konoha."

"I want to . . . be normal."

"If you became Miu Inoue,

you'd get hurt."

"When you write
your novel, let me
read it, okay?"

"Konoha . . . you should write a novel someday."

**I WON'T FORGET—**

# Contents

# BOOK GIRL

*and the Scribe Who Faced God*
*Part 2*

*Mizuki Nomura*
*Illustrations by Miho Takeoka*

Press

NEW YORK

Book Girl and the Scribe Who Faced God, Part 2
Story: MIZUKI NOMURA
Illustration: MIHO TAKEOKA

Translation by Karen McGillicuddy

Bungakushoujo to kami ni nozomu romancier vol. 2
©2008 Mizuki Nomura. All rights reserved.
First published in Japan in 2008 by KADOKAWA CORPORATION ENTERBRAIN
English translation rights arranged with KADOKAWA CORPORATION ENTERBRAIN
through Tuttle-Mori Agency, Inc., Tokyo.

English translation © 2014 by Hachette Book Group, Inc.

Yen Press
Hachette Book Group
237 Park Avenue, New York, NY 10017

www.HachetteBookGroup.com
www.YenPress.com

Yen Press is an imprint of Hachette Book Group, Inc. The Yen Press name and logo are trademarks of Hachette Book Group, Inc.

First Yen Press Edition: January 2014

Library of Congress Cataloging-in-Publication Data

Nomura, Mizuki.
    [Bungakushoujo to kami ni nozomu romancier. English]
    Book Girl and the scribe who faced God. Part 2 / Mizuki Nomura ; illustrations by Miho Takeoka ; translation by Karen McGillicuddy. — First Yen Press edition.
        pages cm. — (Book Girl ; 8)
    Originally published in Japan in 2008 by Kadokawa Corporation Enterbrain, Tokyo, under title: Bungakushoujo to kami ni nozomu romancier.
        ISBN 978-0-316-07698-2 (pbk.)
    [1. Mystery and detective stories.    2. Books and reading—Fiction.    3. Goblins—Fiction.
    4. Japan—Fiction.]    I. Takeoka, Miho, illustrator.    II. McGillicuddy, Karen, translator.    III. Title.
    PZ7. N728Bns 2014
    [Fic]—dc23
                                                                        2013029959

10 9 8 7 6 5 4 3 2 1

RRD-C

Printed in the United States of America

and the Scribe Who Faced God
Part 2

There's a story I want to write, Kana.

It's a sweet story, one that will instantly make any stomach full, no matter how empty, white and pure like the manna that rained down on the people who wandered the desert.

God poured manna down on them, gave them hope, and kept demonstrating his unwavering love until they reached the promised land.

It would be so nice, Kana, if I could write a gentle, happy story like that someday.

And if I did, Kana?

Do you think I would be able to confess everything I ought to, beg your forgiveness, and go through that narrow gate with courage?

## Prologue—Memories for an Introduction: the Last Thing She Whispered

To you whom I loved as much as this, good-bye.

There was a girl who, with those words, parted from the person she loved best.

If she loved him, then why couldn't they be together?

Why did she need to so gently shake free of the hand she'd held?

Why did she turn her back on him when he was gazing at her in despair, and then move toward the narrow gate all alone?

Could they not have walked together hand in hand, on a broad, bright road?

When I was seventeen, her words and her behavior seemed inexplicable to me and simply made me sad. I couldn't accept it.

Good-bye.

Around the same time, the person who had educated me fixed me with a clear gaze and she, too, whispered that word inside a shower of pure white flower petals.

\*      \*      \*

Good-bye.

It was a warm smile, melting into the gentle, golden light of sunset, that resurfaced in my aching chest.

Slender shoulders; delicate limbs; long, wispy braids swaying.

Her back never turning around.

Her voice, so gentle it was heartbreaking, echoing again and again in my ears.

Good-bye.

You were more important to me than anyone.

# Chapter 1—The Murderous Desire You Trigger in Me

"Here you go. Like I promised."

When I slowly dropped the peach-colored phone strap of the woven ball into her palm, Kotobuki's face curved into a joyful smile.

"Th-thanks."

"Sorry it's so late," I apologized a tiny bit sheepishly, and she shook her head so violently it sent her hair flying.

"No way! It's really cute!"

She squeezed it with a little smile, and then she slooowly opened her hand again, picked it up in her fingertips, and dangled it in front of her face. She went on gazing at it, enchanted.

The morning classroom was filled with an easy atmosphere. Clear light streamed in from the windows, making Kotobuki's face shine brightly.

People would start filtering into the classroom in greater numbers soon, but it looked like Kotobuki wasn't paying attention. She looked up at me and her cheekbones were ever so slightly pink.

"Did...you hold on to this phone strap the whole time?"

"Yeah. It was supposed to be a souvenir from my trip over the summer, but I forgot to give it to you. Like that postcard you were supposed to send me over the summer."

When I said that, she pursed her lips a little.

"Come on. I mean…you thought I was an awful person. You hated me."

"That's not true. In fact, it was more like *you* hated *me*. So I thought you might not like it if I brought you a souvenir."

"B-but no! I didn't hate you, it's just—I-I would get nervous and look really intimidating—even when I tried to talk to you, the words didn't come out very well, and—hate you? No way. I mean, this whole time I've—"

It was cute how she was denying it so frantically, and the inside of my chest felt ticklish. Feeling happy, I laughed.

"I know that now."

When I said that, Kotobuki's face calmed as well, and she dropped her head shyly. "Good."

She squeezed the phone strap in both hands, cradling it.

"You picked this out for me."

"I did."

"Were you thinking about me when you chose it?"

"Yeah. I thought this color would suit you."

Kotobuki looked even more embarrassed, the corners of her mouth relaxing, and in a tiny voice, she whispered, "I…like pink."

Then, her cheeks still red, she asked, "But what made you think to buy me a souvenir? I was so off-putting back then."

She glanced up at me, her eyes charged with expectation.

My voice stuck.

Something bitter had mingled suddenly with my glowing, treacly emotions.

—*Because Tohko said we should buy souvenirs for everyone.*

Smiling kindly, using a tone like an older sister worrying about

6

her little brother, she said it was important to build up plenty of little gestures for the people I talked to every day.

With a scratchy sensation deep in my chest, I opened my mouth to speak.

"Because I started yelling and left so suddenly that time I went to visit you in the hospital. It was to make up for that…"

I saw Kotobuki was disappointed, and I hurried to add, "And then I thought it would be great if I could get to know you better because of it."

Instantly, a syrupy light came into her eyes. Kotobuki turned to one side in embarrassment.

"Y-you don't have to lie. I'm just happy that you bought it for me and held on to it all this time."

The word *lie* sent a stab through me.

But—

"I'll treasure it forever."

Kotobuki lifted her face and smiled, and instantly my clenched heart was filled once more with something gentle.

Her pure, straightforward eyes devoid of any betrayal or scheming, simply intent, looking only at me—

I'd been saved by those eyes.

When I returned home from Ryuto's house yesterday at my lowest point, Kotobuki had been the one who held and supported me as I cried.

*"You don't have to write anymore.*

*"…Even if you don't write novels…I'll stay with you."*

As fat tears rolled down my face, she told me that. I had felt indescribably elated.

Until then, I'd thought that I would never feel for Kotobuki the intense emotions that I'd had for Miu.

But when I was with Kotobuki, courage welled up in me. The

tenderness I felt toward her awkward kindness, toward her rough and fervent words, came from the heart.

Reminiscent of exactly the calm, peaceful life that I wanted.

If I was with Kotobuki, I could be stronger.

So I wasn't going to lose my way. It didn't matter if I never became an author.

If I could walk unhurriedly down the broad path that everyone took, under a bright sun, smiling with Kotobuki, supporting each other, still Konoha Inoue, I knew I would have no greater joy.

"You want to go home together today?"

"Sure." She nodded and then shifted her eyes away in embarrassment. "Oh, Mori's here with everyone. I'm gonna go now, okay?"

She gave a little wave and then moved away while stealing glances back at me. It was adorable.


"You guys look like you've relaxed a lot."

When I turned around, Akutagawa's eyes were soft.

"I was worried, since you've been out of school."

"I'm sorry…Thank you for worrying about me so much. And for bringing Miu out."

"Oh, I was just an escort. It was Asakura's idea to go see you."

Akutagawa's easy smile touched his mature lips.

Miu and Akutagawa had both helped me for sure…

When we parted ways at the coffee shop, I hadn't had a clue what I should do. I'd felt empty and on the verge of snapping. But today I could tell Akutagawa how I felt and be honest.

"No, I was glad when you told me to stop and think. Thanks to you, I finally found an answer," I declared cheerfully. "I'm not going to be an author after all. I'm not writing any more novels."

In contrast to my buoyancy, the smile disappeared from Akutagawa's face and his expression grew slightly uneasy.

"I see...If that's what you've decided, it's not my place to say anything. But are things going to be okay with Sakurai?"

Instantly the skin on my entire body prickled, as if something cold had been pressed to the back of my neck.

Ryuto!

Like those of a ferocious wild dog, his eyes grew until my mind filled with a rush of fresh, bright red blood, and the sound of his voice whispering over the phone echoed in my ears.

*"So Kotobuki's gonna be a problem...huh?"*

His low voice charged with irritation.

*"If you don't break up, I dunno what I'm gonna do. I might mess her up bad and break her."*

He'd said it coldly, thickly, spelling out each word to make sure I understood.

I'd called him back on his cell phone immediately after. But no matter how many times I tried, I only got his voice mail and never got hold of him.

If something really were to happen to Kotobuki...My guts twisting with worry, I called Kotobuki's cell phone.

*"Inoue? What's wrong?"*

As soon as I heard the surprise in her voice, I sank to the floor with relief.

*"I was worried about you."*

*"C'mon, it's still early. I'm fine."*

*"How much farther to your house?"*

*"Um, about thirty minutes?"*

"*Let's talk until you get there, then.*"

"*Wha—? Okay!*"

"*And let's go to school together tomorrow, too.*"

"H-hold on. *This is so—did something happen, Inoue?*" Koto-buki had asked in a rush, concern in her voice.

"*I want to be with you.*"

I said it with such anxiety in my voice that she was silent for one second, then two, then—

"*O-okay. If that's what you want, okay,*" she'd whispered bluntly, embarrassed.

I kept on talking, as if a dark shadow were hunting me, until Kotobuki reached home.

After we hung up, my hand had been cold and stiff, and my entire body was soaked in sweat.

I called Ryuto's phone again several times after that, but never got hold of him. Each time I was connected to his voice mail, my heart leaped and then a shiver went down my spine.

When I lay down in bed, I saw only bad visions and I was seized several times by the impulse to call Kotobuki and make sure she was safe.

Even when morning finally came, I was in no mood to savor my breakfast slowly and I arrived at our meeting spot thirty minutes early.

I waited, stomping my feet and breathing in white clouds, when through the mist of morning, Kotobuki appeared with my white scarf wound around her neck. My nostrils flared and I thought I might cry.

*Inoue...*

Bashful, Kotobuki had called out to me, her cheeks as red as apples, her eyes shining vibrantly. She seemed very happy.

The instant I saw that look on her face, I felt as if a heavy stone that had been slung across my shoulders had melted away into nothing.

Thank god.

Thank god Kotobuki was here.

I'd been so anxious, but just having Kotobuki walking beside me, my nerves eased and my heart grew stronger.

That was how we arrived at school.

The courage Kotobuki had given me still lingered in my heart, supporting me firmly.

I couldn't believe that Ryuto had said those words as an idle threat.

Whenever I remembered the voice he'd uttered them in, his face filled with madness, my body shrank even now. Anxiety caressed my heart like a knife.

I had to protect Kotobuki.

"I have a favor to ask, Akutagawa."

I confessed that I thought Ryuto might do something to Kotobuki.

Akutagawa's face grew steelier as I watched.

"I'm going to be with Kotobuki as much as I can until I can talk to Ryuto, but would you mind keeping an eye on her, too?"

"No problem."

"Thank you. I've asked a lot of favors from you lately. Sorry."

"It's fine. You almost waited too long to ask. You take on too much on your own. I'm not too perceptive, so if you don't say something early on, I can't help."

He said it with an earnest face, and though I was happy, I was also baffled.

"…I think you try to do everything on your own more than I do, Akutagawa."

"I don't mean to…"

Akutagawa knit his brows. I smiled warmly.

"If you insist, then. If you run into any problems, tell me, okay? I'm not that observant, either."

When I said that, Akutagawa's face softened. "Sure."

The bell rang and everyone went back to their seats in a flurry. I started to walk back to mine, too.

"Inoue."

"Yeah?"

I stopped and turned around. After a hesitant look passed through his eyes, Akutagawa asked, "...Did you and Amano talk things out?"

My chest pinched tight.

Akutagawa was looking at me, pained. It struck me that he was reflecting exactly what was on my own face.

"I'm glad that you chose the path of not writing and that you're prepared to get into it with Sakurai. But won't that mean things are going to get even worse with you and Amano?"

The words stuck in my throat, my breathing grew strained, and I couldn't answer. I couldn't meet Akutagawa's gaze fully.

Our teacher came in, and we both turned our eyes away and sat at our desks.

*"...Did you and Amano talk things out?"*

The suffocating feeling continued throughout class, as if my throat were blocked up. Akutagawa's words lingered in my mind.

I hadn't made a decision on my relationship with Tohko yet.

The thing she had wanted from me.

That I would write the story her dead mother should have written.

But that was impossible.

I wasn't Tohko's mother and I couldn't write the story Tohko was hoping for.

These past few days, I'd found out a lot about Tohko. That her father had been an editor. That her mother had ambitions of being an author. That they had both died in a car accident. About the relationship between the Amanos and Ryuto's mother, Kanako. How Kanako treated Tohko, the memento of her friends.

How Tohko had lived in Kanako's house.

*"She looks unfriendly, but she's actually a nice person. She let me live here. She's really a good person."*

*"Welcome home, Aunt Kanako!"*

Tohko, her feverish body recovering from illness, greeting Kanako at the door as if she was overjoyed to see her.

The author Kanako Sakurai, who had silently gone by Tohko without as much as a glance in her direction.

I'd been unable to do anything that day.

Anger had surged into me, making the blood in my body boil; my chest had hurt as if it were tearing itself apart; I'd been filled with a desire to scream—and yet I'd been unable to give voice to a single word.

I'd been unable to do anything at all for Tohko.

*"Those two…are always like that. Tohko says somethin' and Kanako ignores her. It's been that way ever since… Tohko came to stay at our house."*

I'd been unable to tell her how bizarre it was to smile at someone treating you like you don't exist when you're right in front of them. I was so angry I was shaking—and yet I'd been unable to say it. And I hadn't been able to say to Kanako, *Why do you ignore Tohko? Don't you think you're taking things a little far when she's lived in the same house as you for so many years?*

Tohko and Kanako had created their own world in that cramped space, one just for the two of them, and I'd been unable to enter it, as if I were merely reading words printed in a book.

*"You're the one who let her dream, and now you're runnin' away?"*

*"You gotta write, Konoha."*

Ryuto had said that if I wrote, something would change. That I was Tohko's author.

I couldn't answer that plea.

Not even if Tohko had been at my side, holding my hand whenever I started to cry and helping me to stand back up for the last two years, hoping for exactly that.

It was thanks to Tohko that I'd managed to come this far despite stumbling so many times.

But I couldn't grant Tohko's wish.

I couldn't become an author and I couldn't write a novel! Even if it meant I was ungrateful, even if it meant I was selfish, that was the one thing I couldn't do!

I couldn't!

I felt like I was losing my mind with the pangs that seemed to beat against my skull. Tohko had betrayed me.

But I had betrayed Tohko, too. Tohko who had unfailingly given me more warmth and kindness than I could measure.

It was probably because I wore such a gloomy expression that Akutagawa apologized to me during the break.

"Sorry. I didn't mean to make you agonize over it."

"It's okay. Tohko and I...we're done."

Done—I guess that's what we were.

Because we weren't going to see each other again?

Because we would become memories to each other and grow apart?

If we could forget, great. But *could* I forget when Tohko's memory lingered so vividly in my eyes, in my ears, on my skin? When my chest ached so much I could hardly bear it?

Akutagawa laid a hand on my shoulder without a word.

"If it makes you look so pained, why not go see Amano? Wasn't she important to you? She always cared about you. She thought well of you.

"Maybe it's not my place to say this. But I still think Amano was probably the one who understood you best."

Akutagawa's straightforward gaze was right in front of me. Fighting back the pain that tightened my throat, I whispered, feeling like I could cry, "Yeah...you might be right."

The one who understood me best.

And yet she'd ordered me to write a novel. Told me to go back to being Miu Inoue.

Even though she should have known how much I would loathe that. Had she wished it so hard that she couldn't help but say it?

To read a novel like manna, like her mother should have written—a story as sacred as nourishment from God—sweet and white, falling from heaven.

Wanting to fill her empty stomach with it.

"I'm ashamed, but...there's nothing I can do for Tohko. Because what Tohko needs is me as an author. If all I am is a high school student...I can't help her."

My heart chafed.

Akutagawa was looking at me impatiently.

Behind me, Kotobuki called out, "Inoue!"

15

Her shy, quiet voice erased my bleak emotions. I smiled and said, "See you," then walked over to her.

And so several days went by.

I waited for Kotobuki in the morning and at the end of the day so we could go to school and leave together. Even after we got home, we would talk on our cell phones or text, then call each other again and send texts after we hung up, then finally tell each other "good night" over the phone. We spent the time feeling close, even though we were apart.

I was always on high alert about what Ryuto was planning out there, but the peaceful days went on so long that I started to lower my guard.

When I saw Takeda in the hall and asked, "How's Ryuto doing?" she told me in a bright voice, "He's good. We had a *feast* at Harumi's restaurant yesterday."

Harumi's restaurant was the place we'd had the Christmas Eve party. Ryuto went there all the time. Harumi was a pretty waitress who worked there.

"We ran into four girls and it turned into all-out hand-to-hand combat. Ryu got slapped *plus* he got splattered with a glass of soda with ice in it."

She told me this with a guileless smile, as if she were engaging in perfectly ordinary conversation.

"Were you...a part of that, Takeda?"

"No, I watched and had some of their new ginger cake."

"...Oh. There hasn't been anything else out of the ordinary?"

"Um...well, Ryu's been calling someone a lot. I guess they never pick up, though, and he gets a little annoyed."

"Calling someone? Who?"

"I dunno." She beamed with a meaningful expression. "Are you worried about Nanase? That maybe Ryu's still tormenting her?"

"Yeah. I want to protect her."

When I said that, Takeda's face suddenly turned serious.

"You've changed toward Nanase a little, Konoha."

"Wh—y-you think so?"

"Yup. I feel like you cherish Nanase more than you did before. And I think Nanase's started to be less uptight when she's with you."

"Was I that rude to her before?"

"Nooo. Nanase was all hyperaware of you, but you were toootally cool. Did you feel sorry for her?"

"Urk…"

It was true.

Takeda grinned again.

"I'm glad things look like they're going well. I gotta go."

I watched her wave and move off, in a complex frame of mind.

The part about Ryuto calling someone nagged at me. She said he looked annoyed. If it was some girl he was messing around with, fine, but…

Contrary to how placidly my days were slipping by, the dark clouds looming in my heart refused to clear away. I knew Ryuto hadn't given up yet. He seemed likely to do anything right now, no matter how horrible, as long as it would achieve his goal. And that scared me.

It was lunchtime when Maki spoke to me.

"Haven't seen you in a while, Konoha."

I was picking out some bread for lunch at the school store, and I turned around in surprise.

She was smiling sexily, giving off the impression of a brilliant rose blooming proudly in a peaceful field or of a carnivorous flower. Her enchanting brown hair spilled over her ample chest in waves.

17

I had always seen Maki in her workroom in the music hall before, so this situation in front of the school store at lunchtime was so incongruous that it left me stunned.

With a look that told me everything was clear to her, Maki asked, "I heard you came to see me. Was that about Tohko, by any chance?"

When I twitched, her eyes narrowed with a smile that said, "I thought so." "We can't relax here. Let's go to my workroom." She walked off with an arrogant bearing, as if it were foregone that I would follow.

When we reached her workroom, Takamizawa had set out tea and sandwiches.

"So? You wanted to ask me something?"

Feeling suffocated, I opened my mouth. "How much do you know?"

"Just about everything that can be found out," she answered offhandedly.

"What about Tohko's parents?"

"They died in a car accident, right? When Tohko was eight."

"Okay, what about Ryuto's mother?"

"She's that author, Kanako Sakurai. She sure is famous, huh? *For a lot of reasons.*"

The insides of my mouth dried out and prickled. In a hoarse voice, I asked the thing I wanted to know most of all.

"Do you think Kanako poisoned Tohko's parents like she wrote in her novel?"

As soon as I spoke the words, the pit of my stomach grew heavy as a rock and my fingertips became cold as ice.

A bewitching smile came over Maki's face.

"The police investigation found no evidence that Kanako Sakurai had murdered the Amanos. The circumstances of the accident were unusual, though, so it's possible to imagine there was some crisis while they were driving.

"They had left Tohko at Kanako's house that day in order to attend a wedding. Ryuto had stayed the night with them, and after the family had breakfast at their apartment together, they took Tohko and Kanako's son, Ryuto, to the Sakurai house. Then they headed to the ceremony in a car driven by Fumiharu, the husband.

"If Kanako poisoned them, it would have happened then, but..."

Maki cut her words off for effect. I held my breath.

"But Kanako wasn't in the house then. The one who met them at the door was the housekeeper, who was watching the house while Kanako was gone. So, barring her using some sort of trick, it's impossible for Kanako to have poisoned them."

Cold sweat poured down beneath my clothes.

Kanako hadn't poisoned the Amanos.

So then why had Kanako written a novel in which she seemed to confess to killing them?

Why had she treated Tohko as if she didn't exist?

Had she taken her in, intending to ignore her all along?

I recalled what the letter from Kanako that I'd read in Tohko's room had said, and I shuddered.

*"I wonder if you think things would be better if I were dead."*

The letter that she had written to Yui, supposedly her best friend.

Kanako had accused Yui of having poison and of intending to poison her husband, Fumiharu, and Kanako with it.

*"Once you've killed him, are you going to kill me, too? Are you going to poison my food...?"*

Kanako knew where the poison was hidden, too; when she checked, there was the poison.

The terror and suspicion that had been born when I read the letter rose again and bit into my heart, although I beat it back again and again.

Had Yui been the one who poisoned them?

Had she forced Fumiharu into a double suicide—?

Ryuto had said it, too.

That *Yui had poison.*

That night when it had seemed the very core of my body would freeze, lit by the eerie light of the moon, as he fixed me with eyes that glinted in their depths, he'd revealed that he was the reincarnation of his father, Takumi Suwa.

That he had pressed the violet, heart-shaped bottle of poison into Yui's hands. That Yui had smiled ecstatically and thanked him. And that she had used it.

*"After all, the only way you can hold on to the person you love forever is to either kill yourself or kill them, right?"*

I recalled his low, sweet voice, rich with madness, and it gave me goose bumps.

There was no such thing as reincarnation! If he was saying that and he meant it, then Ryuto was insane. And yet there was a bizarre, undeniable code in his words.

*"Please write, Konoha. Before I give Tohko Ole Lukøje's little violet bottle."*

I had glimpsed the same name in Kanako's letter.

*"The stories you wrote were just like the dreams Ole Lukøje gave to children with his painted umbrella. Insubstantial and ambiguous, leaving no impression, they disappear the moment morning comes."*

Ole Lukøje was a fairy of sleep who appears in a fairy tale by Hans Christian Andersen. Was this repetition of names a coincidence? Or was it—

"You don't look so hot."

When I came to my senses, my palms were soaked with sweat. I was sure my face was as pale as someone deathly ill, too.

I let out a short breath to get my breathing under control, and then in a hard voice, I whispered, "I'm fine."

Maki didn't look concerned in the slightest; actually, she seemed to be enjoying the show I was giving her.

Even when I showed weakness, this girl had no sympathy. Instead, all she did was look down her nose at me.

"There's nothing wrong. At all."

"Oh, really?"

Her lips pulled into a mean-spirited smile.

"Actually, I heard *you* were under the weather and that you were at home resting. Are you better now?"

Still smiling, Maki answered, "Well, I wasn't exactly sick."

Then she rested her elbows on the table jovially, propped her chin in her hand, and peered at me.

"Is there anything else you want to ask me? Today's special. I'll have a chat with you and it won't cost you a thing."

"Ryuto's father, Takumi Suwa...what kind of a person was he?"

"Ho-ho, I've got a perfect tidbit for that one."

Maki's eyes flashed sarcastically.

21

"I've seen pictures of Takumi, and he looks unsettlingly like Ryuto. It's only natural, them being father and son and all, but even so, they're so alike it's as if Takumi himself had crawled out of his grave.

"It seems Ryuto inherited his personality from his father, too. Even though Takumi was still a minor, he worked for nightclubs and scouted for adult entertainment. He was a bum, a blow-off guy who spent his life going around from one girl's house to another apparently. He couldn't stand the battles women got into, and yet he was totally blasé without a hint of self-awareness. Just like the Ryuto Sakurai we know, eh? Father and son, both a total waste."

Maki hated Ryuto, and she was being merciless.

When she said that they looked disturbingly alike, I experienced a sensation as if my chest were being scraped out.

*". . .'Cos I'm the reincarnation of Takumi Suwa."*

I knew it was impossible, but still the image of Takumi Suwa gradually overlapped with Ryuto, was becoming Ryuto, in my mind. Twisting his lips unsettlingly and looking at me with glinting eyes.

"I heard that Takumi died in a car accident, too."

Maki shrugged.

"He jumped out into the road to save a cat. The cat was fine, but he was taken to the hospital in an ambulance and died in surgery."

"A cat?"

"It's a totally unbelievable way to die, right? Jumping in front of a car to protect a cat. What a completely brainless guy. The funeral was packed with women, and I hear it's still the stuff of legend."

She scrunched up her face at the idiocy of it and took a sip of tea.

". . . Did Kanako attend Takumi's funeral?"

Maki set her cup down and answered breezily. "Apparently not. She said she was working on a manuscript at her office. Though I heard Tohko's mom went."

Ryuto's threatening eyes flashed through my mind, and my heart thrummed again.

"How did Kanako feel about Takumi, do you think? She gave birth to Ryuto, so there must have been love, but then to work through his funeral... And when he was in the accident, she didn't go to the hospital. That's what Ryuto—"

Maki looked at me with mocking, sympathetic eyes.

"You are such a child."

Her voice was cold in its declaration and I choked.

"There are women who can have a man's child without being in love."

All of a sudden, I had no words.

It was like Maki were attacking me—the air abruptly gone cold.

At last, I forced my voice out. "So then why did she have him?"

Maki replied, her eyes still resting on me, "It could be... for *revenge*?"

The drastic word stabbed into my chest.

*Revenge?*

Against *who*? Yui? Fumiharu?

"There were rumors that Kanako was having an affair with her editor, Fumiharu Amano, anyway, so it's perfectly believable that she would get together with another man and get pregnant as payback because of that romantic entanglement and that she would have the child."

It couldn't be—

Who would have a child with someone they didn't even love as *payback*?

"That's just my *interpretation*. It's not a fact; it's something I think is plausible."

She teased me, seeming to ask, *Was that too shocking for you, Konoha?* and my cheeks flared with heat.

Her face calm, Maki said, "Let me see your phone," and then she stored her number in it. "If something happens, you can call me. Though I might charge a consultation fee next time."

"...Could I ask you just one other thing?"

"Go right ahead."

"If Tohko's parents were poisoned, is it possible that Takumi was the one who got hold of it for them?"

Maki returned my phone, then replied with a cloying tone of voice.

"Actually, that's the more natural thing to think. Since Takumi had entrée at shady places, he could probably have gotten his hands on some poison. What's surprising is the possibility that Kanako would have gone out with Takumi for that reason."

I felt nauseated and uncomfortable.

I thanked Maki and left the music building. As I was walking down the hallway, various images and words swirled in my mind.

Had Takumi Suwa really gotten the poison? Had he given it not to Kanako, but to Yui?

No—that was all stuff Ryuto had said. Not facts, just simple delusions. I couldn't get taken in by it. Reincarnation was laughable!

*I know that.*

"*...I have memories from my previous life.*"

"*Things aren't gonna settle down unless someone disappears, just like back then.*"

*　　*　　*

I shook my head fiercely.

Wasn't I supposed to have forgotten about Tohko already?

Had there really been poison? Who had poisoned them? It had nothing to do with me.

Tohko's parents had died nine years ago. There was no use searching for the perpetrator now. Especially if Yui might have done it—

When I got back to my classroom right as the bell was ringing, Akutagawa came up to me.

"You weren't with Kotobuki?"

"Huh?"

"I told her you'd gone to the store and she left."

"She did? I haven't seen her."

"Really...I thought since neither of you were back, I was sure you were together, but..."

Akutagawa's eyes clouded. My heart chilled as well and then ached, as if it were being wrung out.

Was Kotobuki still looking for me?

A chill crept up my spine. I pulled my cell phone out of my pocket and checked the calls. There were zero.

The bell rang and everyone sat down at their desks.

Kotobuki still wasn't back.

Mori, who was friends with Kotobuki, glanced worriedly toward the hall.

Akutagawa, too, wore a grim expression.

I called Kotobuki's phone. A message played telling me she couldn't be reached because either her phone was turned off or she was somewhere with no signal.

In a fog, I sent her a text.

"What happened? Class started. Where are you?"

My pulse quickened and my temples started to ache sharply. Why wasn't Kotobuki back?

My chest was dyed black with worry. Hurry—hurry—come back soon, Kotobuki.

The teacher came into the room.

Kotobuki still wasn't there.

Just then, the phone gripped in my hands buzzed momentarily. There was something incoming.

A text!

But it was from Takeda, not Kotobuki.

Its subject line was "Nanase"—

I shuddered. Frantically, I opened the text and checked what it said under my desk.

library

As soon as my eyes fell on the short, uncapitalized message, I was already standing.

The people at the desks around me turned their faces up in surprise. The teacher's eyes went round, too.

"I'm sorry. I'm going to the nurse's office!" I shouted, sounding like I'd just crossed paths with a brigand, and I flew out of the classroom.

There was no doubt in my mind! Something had happened to Kotobuki!

Had I been careless thinking that he couldn't make a move at school during lunch in the middle of the week?!

*"So Kotobuki's gonna be a problem . . . huh?"*

The look filled with irritation and the chilling, knifelike voice cut again and again into my heart, carving it up.

*"I dunno what I'm gonna do."*

Ryuto murmuring through the phone in a low, grasping voice.

He hadn't been normal that day!

I'd known that, and yet—

Known that Ryuto wouldn't give up for anything. That what he said wasn't a threat: it was the truth.

I'd known that! So then why had I let Kotobuki out of my sight?

I ran desperately through the hall and bolted down the stairs, berating my blunder as I went until my head almost split.

My breathing was rough, and I thought my throat was going to rip open. Sweat ran into my eyes and my feet tangled up and I almost fell over, but I planted my feet and fought it off.

The world around me was warping like rubber.

Please—please let me be in time!

There was a CLOSED sign hanging on the door to the library. Beyond, everything was silent; only my rough panting engulfed my ears. I turned the knob and went inside.

As my shoulders heaved with my breathing, I looked around.

The desk and reading area were both empty.

In that place, a single student sat in a chair at a table, reading a book.

Her cold eyes, devoid of any emotion, looked down at the words, and she turned the pages silently, without a sound. As if a mechanized doll were sitting there—

"Takeda!"

When I called her name, she raised her still-empty eyes to me, then turned her face ever so slightly in the direction of the room in the basement.

I bolted toward it in a daze, opened the door that led downstairs, then descended the spiral staircase so fast that it made me dizzy.

When I pulled open the weighty iron door, the sweet smell

given off by yellowing books and the sharp, cold air pricked at my cheeks and forehead.

The lamp on the small side table lit the room unsettlingly. In the slight space of the dim "book graveyard," two shadows were cast on top of each other.

The lower shadow was kicking its feet, trying desperately to push the upper shadow back.

It was Ryuto and Kotobuki.

I saw that Kotobuki had fallen to her back on the floor and that Ryuto was looming over her. Heat flared from the back of my neck to my ears to the core of my brain.

It was the first time I'd felt rage at another person so strongly that I wanted to murder them. Even the insides of my eyes turned bloodred, my heart went wild, my reason fled, and I became a bundle of emotion. I surged forward.

"Get off her! Stop!"

When Ryuto turned around to look at me, I punched him in the face, grabbed his collar with both hands, and sent him flying back. A mound of books collapsed, hitting Ryuto on the shoulder as they tumbled to the floor. Dust particles floated about in the faint light from the table.

"I-Inoue!"

Kotobuki called my name, her voice thick with tears, and clung to me, trembling. Her hair and uniform were all rumpled and the ribbon over her chest had come untied.

"I'm sorry, Kotobuki. I'm sorry."

I hugged Kotobuki, whispering the words over and over.

Kotobuki didn't stop shaking. She must have been so terrified. She gripped my uniform tightly and pressed her face against my chest and sobbed, "Inoue…Inoue…" White dust was stuck to her lovely brown hair.

Clenching my jaw, I glared sharply at Ryuto.

Ryuto plunked onto his bottom on the floor and looked up at me.

His eyes flashed with displeasure, and his lips were twisted pettily. I saw that and the blood rushed into my head.

"Don't *ever* touch Kotobuki again!! What you're doing is a crime! Why don't you just forget I exist? No matter what you do, I'm not going to write a novel! I won't go back to being Miu Inoue! If you do something to Kotobuki again, I might kill you. That's how I angry I am!"

In a thorny, grating voice, Ryuto muttered, "Never thought I'd hear ya say a word like *kill*. Your girlfriend that important to you? You oughta quit tryin' stuff you're not used to. You and me, Konoha, we're on different levels. I'm used to people tellin' me they're gonna kill me. No matter how much they say it, there's no one...who'll actually do it for me..."

Ryuto pulled a folding knife out of his pocket. He flicked it open and tossed it at my feet.

Then, as if to fan my rage, he hitched his lips up slightly.

"I want you to kill me with that thing. If you don't, I'm gonna do the same thing again, as many times as I want.

"I really am gonna break your precious Kotobuki. She's in my way, after all. I really do want her to just disappear from your life."

Lying on the concrete floor scattered with old books, the blade of the knife gave off a cold light.

My head grew numbingly hot, my throat was bone-dry, and I felt as if I'd been backed up against a cliff edge. A vicious animal was closing in on me steadily, and if I didn't kill him, he'd kill me—that was the urgent feeling that had me under its sway.

Kotobuki tugged on my sleeve uneasily.

"Don't...," she whispered in a halting voice.

Ryuto's voice rang out, as if to eradicate her words.

"Then maybe you want me to tear her up right in front of you?"

Kotobuki flinched and shrank back. I did, too.

He'd fixed on us a look that belonged to a demon, filled with dangerous enthusiasm. Cruel eyes without a shred of familiarity—

"I'm serious. You wanna see which of us would win when we're both bein' serious? C'mon, pick that up and stop my heart. Then I won't tell ya to write ever again. Dead people can't talk. Show my body what it means when you're serious, Konoha."

The silver knife lying at my feet.

If I picked it up and stabbed it into Ryuto's heart, Kotobuki would never be in danger again.

I knew Ryuto wouldn't dodge it.

The air grew thicker and my throat choked tight. I stopped breathing, didn't even blink, looking at the knife.

I couldn't forgive Ryuto for what he'd done to Kotobuki; he wasn't the cheerful Ryuto that he used to be.

If I didn't end it here, the same thing would happen again.

The scene I'd witnessed when I opened the door rose before my eyes again and a bubbling, murderous impulse welled up in me. If I truly wanted to protect Kotobuki—

"Don't!"

As troubling emotions began to drag me in, a forceful voice called me back.

Kotobuki was the one who'd shouted.

Trembling slightly against my chest, gritting her teeth, she glared at Ryuto, her eyes tough, and said loudly, "Inoue's not going to listen to anything you say! A-and I'm—I'm not going to break up with Inoue no matter what you do! This doesn't impress me! I'm not afraid of someone like you! I'm going to be with Inoue for a long time!"

Kotobuki released her grip on my uniform. I watched her crouch down toward the floor, and I started.

"Kotobuki—"

Ryuto's eyes widened, too.

Kotobuki picked up the knife, then hurled it into the shadows where the lines of bookshelves stood. The sound of the knife striking a shelf rang out, then the sound of it falling to the floor, and then silence.

Kotobuki pressed her face against my arm, clinging to it tightly.

"...It was true, what I said before. I care about Inoue...I'm going to stay with him."

What sweet, divine words those were.

My spirit trembled.

Kotobuki lifted her face and smiled at me. It was an awkward smile, but it looked prettier than any other smile could have been.

"Thank you."

I put my arms around Kotobuki's shoulders and pulled her closer. The fire drained out of my body, and I was filled with a feeling of purity. Kotobuki had given me courage yet again.

Ryuto murmured in a frigid voice, "How nice...havin' someone who loves ya like that."

When I looked cautiously over at him, the flaring aura around him had faded and he was looking at us, apparently exhausted.

"But I'm not plannin' on retreatin', either."

Kotobuki tugged at my uniform.

"L-let's go, Inoue."

"Yeah."

I nodded to Kotobuki, then turned toward Ryuto again and said, "I'm not retreating, either. I'm going to protect Kotobuki."

Ryuto was hunkered down, a look of exhaustion still on his face. His powerless, tortured gaze mimicked the face Tohko had shown me when she'd come to my house that one night, and my

chest ached suddenly, but…even so I put my arm around Koto-buki's shoulders and we left the room.

"Inoue! You're okay?"

As soon as I went back up, Akutagawa came running over.

"If one more minute went by and you still weren't back, I was going to run after you."

"Akutagawa—what about class?"

"I left. I said I was going to check on you."

It was all so messed up. The teacher must have been surprised. Kotobuki's eyes were wide, too.

With a bitter look, Akutagawa told us how he'd followed me here and how, when he tried to go downstairs, Takeda had stopped him with the words, *"You should let the people involved talk. Have a seat over there, please."*

Takeda turned a page in her book, pretending ignorance.

"Thank you for telling me about Kotobuki, Takeda."

When I thanked her, she murmured distantly, her eyes still cold, "No problem…"

Takeda didn't ask about what had happened down there or what we'd talked to Ryuto about.

A funny song played in the pocket of Takeda's uniform. Still expressionless, she pulled out her cell phone and checked the screen.

"It's a text…from Ryu."

I flinched.

"What does it say?"

"It says, 'You ratted to Konoha, didn't you?' "

Kotobuki watched Takeda nervously as she typed a reply with practiced movements. Even though she knew about her innocent underclassman's other side, I suppose she still couldn't help being uncomfortable. She gripped my arm fiercely.

My voice hoarse, too, I asked, "What…did you tell him?"

Takeda closed the book she'd just begun reading and stood up. The title on the cover was *No Longer Human*.

"To do it somewhere else next time," she answered coolly, then walked toward the room that led downstairs.

"Takeda! Are you going to Ryuto?"

"Yes. He's pouting, so I'm going to see how he's holding up."

Then she stopped partway there and turned around with the face of the nice, cheerful Chia Takeda.

"I'll see you guys! Later, Konoha, Nanase, Akutagawa!"

The three of us just stood there for a while, struck dumb by the almost blatant transformation.

Finally, Kotobuki broke the silence.

"If—if we all go back to class together, it'll look strange."

"Th-that's true."

"Yeah, you're right."

We spent a few minutes murmuring among ourselves.

In the end, in order to stay consistent, we all went to the nurse's office together.

"Um, I felt a little anemic...I was putting away books in the library and I started to feel dizzy, and then I couldn't move."

"My stomach feels funny. I couldn't get out of the bathroom."

"I'm here to escort Inoue."

That's what we told the nurse.

———⟫◆⟪———

**Has writing made you happy, Kana?**

**Fumiharu has always talked about how writing down a story is an act that brings you closer to God.**

**He said that you had gone through the narrow gate and you were walking toward Him. That he was helping you to reach**

the pinnacle called God. That it was the greatest joy that an editor could have.

But even though you had all that talent and were so pretty and smart and had so much that people wished they had, you didn't look happy to me, Kana.

Fumiharu would say that the thing you truly wanted was somewhere far away and he was sure you would never achieve it.

He said that you were just like Alissa, who sought love in heaven, and that it was that solitude and internal conflict that elevated your writing to another level.

Fumiharu would say these terrible things while cuddling with Tohko with a gentle look on his face, and I would get angry with him.

"It's not true that you can only write novels if you're unhappy."

"You're right. But hunger is important for creation. If Dazai had been content and satisfied, would he have written *No Longer Human*? Without the tragic love of Elise, would *Dancing Girl* have been born? Without the conflict with his father, would Naoya Shiga have been able to write *A Dark Night's Passing*?"

"So then Kana is never allowed to be happy?"

As he swept aside Tohko's bangs with his fingertips, Fumiharu answered quietly, "She can be happy as an author."

As if that was the only way.

## Chapter 2—Poison Dripping from the Hand

I went to school with Kotobuki the next morning, too.

When I told her I would meet her at her house because I was worried about her, she refused vehemently.

"No, don't! Then my whole family will find out I'm going out with you."

"I introduced you to *my* family."

"You told them I was a girl from your class..."

"Th-that's 'cos my mom got this idea that a boy was coming over. Besides, I promised that next time I would do it right and introduce you as my girlfriend."

"Urk. That's true...but you still can't come to my house."

"Even if I introduce myself as just a guy from your class?"

"It's not normal for a guy who's *just* from my class to come all the way to my house in the morning. I said you can't!"

We talked it over heatedly on the phone that night until I broke.

Even so, I was worried, and I got to our meeting spot thirty minutes early. But Kotobuki had gotten there first.

I saw her breathing in white puffs, the scarf I'd given her wound around her neck, and my eyes went wide.

"I wasn't expecting you to be so early, Kotobuki."

"S-so are you. You're here too early!"

I guess she felt awkward because she pursed her lips and turned her face away.

"I just had something else I needed to do and ended up getting here early, that's all."

I held on to my smile and murmured, "Oh, okay. You had something else you needed to do," and Kotobuki peered up at me through her eyelashes. "But that works out, since I came early, too. Now I can be with you that much longer."

When I said that, she turned bright red and murmured quietly, making an excuse, "I swear, it just happened this way. It's not like...I th-thought you might come early or anything..."

"Oh, so that's what it was."

"I said it wasn't!"

Kotobuki had shouted this and whipped her face away again.

"T-today it just happened that I came early, but I might not tomorrow...So you have to come at the time you said you would. I swear I'll be fine. I let my guard down, too, yesterday. I'm being careful so that doesn't happen again. I'm not going to make you worry."

She'd experienced something terrible because of me, but still she was being considerate of me.

My heart clenched sweetly, and I squeezed Kotobuki's hand firmly.

Kotobuki jumped and looked up at me.

"Thanks. Maybe you can't rely on me yet, but I'll be able to protect you eventually. I'll be the one who gets stronger so I don't make *you* worry. I'll work hard at it, so I hope you won't give up on me."

After I said it, I realized something.

*Aha*, this is a sensation I never had when I was with Miu.

Having something I wanted to protect felt so warm and happy.

37

A smile spilled shyly over Kotobuki's face.

"I won't."

Seeing her face, I felt another thrill and warm feelings filled my chest. We started walking, our hands linked.

Even so, that didn't mean I was slacking on my caution about Ryuto.

After we reached the classroom, I reminded Kotobuki, "When you're at school, do everything with someone."

"I will."

"And please put my cell phone number in your speed dial. When Inoue can't pick up the phone, you can call me. I won't mind."

"Thanks, Akutagawa. You should do that, Kotobuki."

"O-okay..."

"I also got some self-defense stuff from my older sister. You can use it if you want."

Akutagawa laid out sprays and alarms and whatever else on his desk with a serious look.

"...Thanks."

Kotobuki didn't seem very into it, but she thanked him and put a bottle of spray and an alarm in her pocket.

Maybe since the three of us were whispering in a tight little clump together for so long—it was so bad that Mori asked me worriedly at lunch, "Hey, are you guys in a threesome? Are you and Akutagawa fighting over Nanase?"

"What?! No way!"

"But yesterday the three of you all skipped class."

"We just went to the nurse's office."

"I think it'd be pretty bad for you if Akutagawa challenged you, but you've got your own qualities. So try not to let Nanase go, okay? For me? I'm rooting for you, Inoue."

She gave me those words of encouragement and then left.

Yet another bizarre misunderstanding...I was sure Mori would interrogate Kotobuki about it, too, and get her all flustered.

That was the extent of the peril (?) and lunch ended without incident.

It was during cleanup after school when Ryuto showed himself.

When I was wiping the window that faced the balcony, I saw Ryuto cutting through the school yard.

I thrust the window open and leaned out. The cold wind buffeted through my hair, stabbing at me. Behind me, a classmate yelled, "Eek! That's cold! Shut the window, Inoue!"

Ryuto was approaching the school building in agitated strides.

My entire body tensed and my throat clenched tight. Was he planning on doing something to Kotobuki again?

The scene in the underground room replayed in my mind, and I thought my body might rip itself apart with rage. I wouldn't let him do anything like that again!

But Ryuto didn't go into the school building; he headed in a different direction.

*Huh?*

The only thing over there was the music hall that belonged to the school orchestra.

Why was he going to the music hall?

Had he come to see Maki, by some chance, and not me?

But Ryuto and Maki were at each other's throats. And I'd heard that just recently Maki had decked Ryuto in the library. That she'd knocked him onto his butt and it had made him sullen—

Still not understanding the situation, unable to ignore it, I closed the window and put my cloth back in its bucket.

Kotobuki was sweeping the floor, talking to Mori and her other friends.

I drew up to Akutagawa, who had been carrying desks, and

whispered in his ear. "Ryuto's here. I'm going to go see what's going on. Can you keep an eye on Kotobuki for me?"

"You gonna be okay on your own?"

Akutagawa furrowed his brow.

"I'll be fine. I need you to worry about Kotobuki instead."

With that, I ran out of the classroom.

I bolted down the hall and headed for the music hall.

The core of my brain was shrouded with a sizzling heat. I didn't think it was possible, but if Ryuto and Maki joined forces, it would be a disaster.

The two of them were identical when it came to brazenly ignoring logic and decency, and they weren't choosy about their methods. Maybe that was why they hated each other so much. On the other hand, you'd expect there to be a lot of common ground between them precisely because they resembled each other so much. If I had to face Ryuto and Maki as enemies simultaneously, things would get scary.

As my chest smoldered with an uneasy premonition, I went into the music hall and climbed up to the workroom where Maki painted her pictures.

Takamizawa was standing in front of the door and he stopped me.

"I'm very sorry. Miss Maki is with a guest."

"Ryuto is in there, isn't he?!"

"I am not at liberty to answer that."

Just as Takamizawa informed me of that in a mild tone, we heard the sound of something breaking and Ryuto yelling angrily from within.

"Gimme a break, lady!"

Takamizawa's face pinched up, as if he thought things were going badly.

"Why didn't you tell me about the baby?! What d'you mean it's none of my business?!"

*Baby?! Whose baby?!*

Ryuto's voice was audible with such force it could have broken the door down.

"That's my baby inside you, right?! So, yeah, that's my business!"

"*You*"—did he mean Maki?!

And "*my baby*"—!

Takamizawa's face looked like he was throwing his hands up in defeat. I opened the door and burst into the room.

There were puddles of water on the floor, and a broken vase, flowers, and even art supplies were scattered flagrantly around the room.

To one side of all that, Ryuto was storming up to Maki.

He was pale, and wild rage and agitation had risen to his popping eyes. He had a threatening air, as if he was on the verge of strangling her.

In contrast, Maki, who wore a work apron over her uniform, was facing Ryuto with a haughty look, as if she was looking down her nose at him.

Still gaping, I asked, "Is that…true? What you just said? That she has your baby inside her?"

They both turned to look at me.

After a brief silence, Maki was the one who spoke.

"It's true that I'm going to have a child."

Her voice was calm and quiet. She proclaimed it with a mature expression that radiated with dignity.

"But this little man has nothing to do with it."

"You bet I do! Who got you pregnant if it wasn't me?! You're not sleepin' with anyone but me, are ya?!" Ryuto shouted, the words like beats of a fist. It was different from the black rage he'd

41

turned on me because of Tohko. It was a fiercer anger, one that flashed into flames more openly.

I was bowled over even more by the raw words he spat out without any hesitation.

"H-hold on! Are you saying—something like *that* happened between you two?"

"There wouldn't be a kid if not, would there?!" Ryuto moaned.

"I guess not, but—Ryuto, aren't you going out with Takeda? I mean, I know you've got tons of girlfriends besides her, but—but—! I didn't think you and Maki got along! Every time you see each other, you trade insults, and then when you went to Maki's estate over the summer, you guys had a huge fight! She kicked you and told you to get out or whatever, and you said you were gone, and—hold on."

Just then my thoughts came to a stop.

I thought back more carefully over the events of the summer.

Ryuto had left the villa as if he'd been driven off by Maki, but during the morning two days later, he'd been walking down the hall with his hair looking as if he'd just taken a shower somehow.

*"Did you stay the night here? Didn't you go into town?"*

*"Y'know, there was all this stuff goin' on."*

That day, an ambiguous, inscrutable smile had come over Ryuto's face, and he had deflected my question.

And then there was Maki...She had appeared in a bathrobe, as if she had just that second gotten out of the bath, and had marks like bugbites on her chest and neck, and it had been incredibly alluring—

Now I recalled that Ryuto had the same marks on his neck, too, and I froze. Had the two of them been together that night?!

42

My cheeks burned and my heart pounded loudly. Then I remembered something even more important.

The night before, I had taken a walk with Tohko to the lake. We saw Yuri and Akira's ghosts there.

But no, Tohko had screamed, "It's a ghooost!" all on her own and ran off, so that's how things wound up, but maybe it hadn't been a ghost—

Maybe the man and woman tangled together naked in the moonlit pond had been—

"R-Ryuto, you two didn't... uh... go for a swim at the lake near the estate over the summer, did you?"

"Yes, we did. We went for a swim and something else, too," Maki answered freely.

My eyes bugged out, and my mouth opened and closed wordlessly.

The two of them really had been together that night!

But Maki, heir to the Himekura Group, a privileged princess to the core who seemed like she had no time for men, had done it outdoors! And with Ryuto of all people!

"So if the baby is from that night, that's almost seven months already!"

I'd heard that babies are born at ten months and ten days. If the birth was premature, it might slip out at seven months. This was bad!

I wasn't the one who was going to give birth or anything, and yet I was rattled.

I looked at Maki's stomach. There was a seven-month-old baby in there—it probably already looked like a person. *Huh?* But Maki's stomach was perfectly svelte. It didn't look like there was a baby in there. I'm sure different people show differently, but was this what a stomach looked like at seven months?

Looking fed up, Maki said, "Calm down, Konoha. It's going to be a long time before I give birth. It's fine."

"Three more months is nothing!"

Maki sighed in exasperation. "Three months is three months, but I'm not giving birth in three months. I just *started* the third month."

"Huh?" My jaw dropped. "It's not from the summer?"

"No."

"Then it's not Ryuto's baby."

As soon as I said it, Ryuto wailed.

"That *is* my kid! Third month means it was that one time, right? Or maybe that other time? Dammit, you said it was okay!"

"*What* was okay?! Are you saying you've been seeing each other that often?! It wasn't just one time over the summer because you got confused?"

Agh, *Did you do it? Did you?* I feel like I've been babbling about embarrassing stuff for too long now.

"I'll leave that to your imagination," Maki stated bluntly, as if it was nothing.

I felt as if I was about to collapse.

Ryuto bit down fiercely on his lip and glared at Maki with wild eyes that were filled with rage. Uneasiness and perplexity steadily colored his expression. He squeezed his fists so tight that his nails must have been digging into his hands, then whispered in a muffled, rasping voice, "... You gonna have it?"

His face looked tortured, as if he was desperately holding up under a pain that threatened to drive him crazy. The next moment his face twisted intensely, he howled, and then shouted, "I said, 'You gonna have it?'! You gonna have that *thing* in your belly?! Answer me, Princess!"

Maki looked at Ryuto with a straight, unfaltering expression, then coldly said, "That is none of your business. This is my problem."

Ryuto's face drew tight.

Maki's voice echoed majestically in the quiet workroom. Her face and tone of voice were almost heartlessly clipped.

"I'm the only one who's going to make decisions about myself. Now and for the rest of my life. So leave."

Ryuto made a face like he was about to cry; then a shudder ran through his shoulders, and his eyes became wild and filled with rage once more, and he growled, "...Don't have it. You *cannot* have it!! It's—that kid is—"

His voice was stretching higher and higher, his eyes sparked, and he made a grab at Maki. Takamizawa had stood silently until then, but he put Ryuto into a full nelson and pulled him away from her.

"I'm very sorry. I need to ask you to leave for today."

Takamizawa was slender and gave an impression of being more intellectual than anything else, so it didn't seem like he'd be that strong, and yet Ryuto was unable to free himself from his hold. His face twisted.

And so he was dragged out of the room.

"Maki! You don't know what you're doin'! I'm not gonna let you have that kid! I swear it!"

His howling voice grew distant until it finally disappeared.

I was utterly stupefied and could do nothing but stand there.

"So? What was it you wanted, Konoha?"

When Maki spoke to me, I came back to my senses.

Maki was looking at me with a smirk.

"Wh—no, I...I saw Ryuto and followed him. And then I... I'm—I'm sorry."

"You don't have to apologize. You would have found out anyway. Just don't tell Tohko about it yet, okay? It would just make her angry, I'm sure."

How could she be this calm? Graduation was looming, but she was still in high school, and plus I was sure Maki's family was incredibly strict.

"I won't tell anyone."

"Thank you."

Maki looked no different than usual. It was only when her lips softened into a smile and she gently rested her right hand over her stomach that a shudder went up my spine.

Even after I left the music hall, I was confused and my feet wobbled unsteadily.

Maki and Ryuto had been getting together and now they had a child—I wondered if Maki intended to have it.

I remembered how she'd told me yesterday, *"There are women who can have a man's child without being in love,"* and my breathing grew strained.

*"It could be... for* revenge?"

My heart chilled, as if someone had pressed ice against it.

No, Maki hadn't been talking about herself. No matter how much she disliked Ryuto, I didn't think she had a reason for something like revenge...

But if Maki went ahead and had the baby, what would Ryuto do? He'd told her not to have it, with that tortured look on his face—Ryuto wasn't happy to have a child. In fact, he seemed terrified, seemed to hate it. And what about Takeda?

There were only a few people left in the classroom. Akutagawa and Kotobuki had waited for me, and they looked nervous.

"Inoue!"

"Did you talk to Sakurai?"

"Are you okay? You look out of it. Did Sakurai hit you in the head or something?"

"I'm fine," I said, evading her question. "I didn't manage to... talk to Ryuto. But I'm pretty sure he didn't come here to do anything to us."

"How come?"

"Uh...he seemed pretty busy with girl problems."

When I told them that, Kotobuki and Akutagawa both gaped at me.


Akutagawa went to his club and I left school with Kotobuki.

I went with her on a shopping trip; then afterward we got a drink at a fast-food place and talked.

Occasionally I would remember about Maki and Ryuto and—

"Geez, you're spacing out again."

There were occasions when Kotobuki pursed her lips curtly, and I would hastily apologize, but...

We passed some time amicably, and after I'd seen Kotobuki off, I went home, too.


"Welcome home, Konoha. One of your friends is here."

"Huh? Who?"

I saw the basketball shoes next to the door and cocked my head to one side. These probably weren't Akutagawa's shoes...

"It's Ryuto."

"What?! Ryuto?!" I shouted, shocked.

"He's been waiting in your room for you this whole time. Poor thing."

"P-poor thing?"

Thrown off by my mother's strangely intense feelings, I climbed the stairs and entered my room.

"Ryuto? I'm coming in."

I opened the door. When I did, the smell of alcohol hit my nose.

"Yer late, Konoha," Ryuto said in a loud, upbeat voice, sitting cross-legged on my floor. His eyes were bleary and his cheeks were red. Several empty cans of beer lay on the table and carpet. There were even bottles of whiskey and brandy, and even those had broken seals!

"Ryuto, you're not old enough to drink!"

He didn't look it at all, but I was pretty sure he was younger than me.

"Don't be so hard on me, okay? You sure are uptight, ain'cha, Konoha?"

Ryuto waved around the whiskey bottle he was holding, and I moved in from the side to swipe it from him.

"If you want to get wasted, do it at your own house. Why are you here?"

With what he'd done to Kotobuki, blustering around without any consideration for me, then getting drunk in my house—I didn't get it.

When I got angry and spoke to him in a strong voice, his eyes suddenly became melancholy and uncertain and his head dropped.

"Are you gonna say that to me, Konoha?" he asked in a whisper, his shoulders slumped.

"Are you kidding me? Did you forget what you've done to me?"

"...You're a cold one, Konoha."

"Excuse me?"

"...You take forever to come home, for one thing."

"We didn't make any plans. You just barged in here."

"...The alcohol's not even that strong."

"Then don't drink it! I mean, you're underage! You have to be twenty to drink!"

"...It's your fault I drank so much."

"Everything you've said to me so far has been a total joke."

Suddenly Ryuto's shoulders shook dramatically. Shockingly, he seemed to be crying. Salty drops pattered onto his knees.

It was bizarre seeing a man burlier than me sobbing like a child. Even more so, the terrifying guy who until very recently had tenaciously pursued me with eyes flashing like a wild dog's. Now he was crying defenselessly.

"... You wouldn't kill me, Konoha—even though you might as well kill me if you don't wanna write—

"Nobody'll kill me. Everyone tosses me aside. Maki'd never tell me she cares about me or loves me—does that mean she only wants my body? All she wanted was my sperm?"

"H-hold on, Ryuto—"

I wish you wouldn't say that so loudly. There's a girl in elementary school in my house, too.

"My mom is going to come if you aren't quiet."

"Ah, she's great. Your mom's so bubbly and nice, and she's great at cooking...nngh...She's really great. A kid would have to be happy being born to a mother like that. Your mom is kinda like Aunt Yui. I used to wish I was born to Yui...If I had been, I woulda eaten tons of great food every day, she woulda patted me on the head and hugged me and been able to say stuff like, 'Have a good day,' or 'Welcome home,' with a smile, and I woulda been crazy happy. I woulda been able to call Yui mom..."

"Ack, hey, Ryuto...!"

He came at me, clinging to me, and I reeled back. Ryuto circled his hand around the back of my neck in a steel grip and sobbed, his breath stinking of alcohol.

"God...why did Jerome love Alissa, y'think? Wasn't Juliette a thousand times better than that joyless stuck-up cow? Juliette was in love with Jerome even. All that moron did was tag after Alissa, tryin' to get with her. Even though Alissa was cold and egotistical and spun up some crazy justification for herself and went through the narrow gate alone to go to God, that horrible, selfish woman."

"R-Ryuto—that hurts. Don't squeeze so hard. And you reek of alcohol. Don't get your face so close—ugh, you're heavy."

When I tried to push him off, he clung to me harder instead and wailed.

"That's how Alissa pushed Jerome away, too! She had the nerve to tell him, 'Don't taint our love,' actin' like a saint. Wasn't she the one who was taintin' it?!

"But Jerome wouldn't quit moonin' over her. What a total idiot."

Ryuto snuffled grandly. Ugh, he got snot on my uniform...

"Did you know that the guy who wrote *Strait Is the Gate* was gay? He married his cousin Madeleine, and they were together forty years, but he never touched her!

"He loved her, but he wrote in his diary about how he felt no desire for a refined lady like her, without givin' her a second thought.

"He published memoirs about how he liked men, or about how he did it out in a field on a trip he took, or a story about how he went with Oscar Wilde, who was a famous pederast, to buy a little boy together. He killed a character in one of his stories that was pretty obviously modeled on Madeleine. He did whatever he wanted. He'd write just about anythin' about his private life in his diary or his novels, and the feelings he wrote about are the most thoughtless ones.

"They say Alissa and Jerome are modeled on Madeleine and Gide, too. The way she's his cousin and two years older than him and the way she turned down Gide's marriage proposal are exactly the same. But Madeleine wasn't as selfish as Alissa. She was reserved and kind—she was a lovin' wife, but Gide wrote it the way he wanted it to be! And then Alissa became a selfish woman who chooses God and casts Jerome aside.

"Alissa's cruel, but Gide is the worst. You agree! Don'cha, Konoha?"

I helplessly, emptily murmured, "Yeah, you're right," patting Ryuto on the back as I said it.

What was I *doing*?

How had I been reduced to comforting the guy who'd been threatening me mercilessly up until yesterday?

Ryuto buried his face against my neck and wept.

The thing with Maki had really upset him...

I recalled the frigid reaction I'd seen Maki give him in the workroom, and it made me sympathize with Ryuto a little.

If I'd been tossed out like that, I'd probably want to cry, too. Though with Ryuto, there was a little bit of just deserts involved.

"...They're all awful. Gide an' Alissa an' Jerome an' Princess Himekura, too.

"The reason Maki did all that with me was to rebel against her family.

"By goin' out with me, she just wanted to prove that she wasn't gonna do whatever they told her to, since I don't fit in with them at all. She used me."

Yeah, that might be part of it...

From what I'd glimpsed of the situation in Maki's family at her estate over the summer...I recalled her relationship with her grandfather, who ruled with absolute authority, and I had to agree.

Maki seemed like she wanted to be free of the Himekura family.

"—Chee doesn't care about me, either," Ryuto proclaimed between sobs. "After Maki chased me off, I went to Chee's class, but she'd already left with her friends."

"Well, that...she can't help that. You guys didn't have plans to meet up or anything."

"But when I called her and told her I wanted to see her, she said she couldn't 'cos she was gonna go see a movie with her friends. And then she hung up! She was like, we were together a whole bunch yesterday, so I'm gonna pass today—even though her man was hurtin' so bad and torn up and puttin' out the SOS!"

He seemed genuinely in despair somehow. I was fed up.

"Y'know…it's wrong to try to get Takeda to comfort you. If you tell her you got another girl pregnant and she was mean to you—any normal girl would get mad and break up with you. Well, Takeda might be forgiving about it, but…"

"I mean, she doesn't care no matter who I go out with, so she'd be able to just *watch* a blowup with another woman totally calmly. Chee doesn't wanna tie me down or monopolize me or nothin' like that. Even though I told her that she could if she wanted… Even if it is just pretend, she's my girlfriend, so she oughta at least be nice at a time like this. Even if it *is* a lie! I care about *her*! And I care about Maki, too. But it doesn't even matter."

"Whaaaa—? Really? You care about Maki?"

"I do. That wrong?"

"I, uh, didn't mean—"

But he cared about Takeda, and he cared about Maki, and he cared about Amemiya, who had passed away, and he probably cared about other girls, too. He just had too big of a heart.

I couldn't handle the fact that he had no sense of guilt.

Ah, but…

Takeda had said as much.

That there was someone special that Ryuto truly cared about. That he couldn't have that person and so everyone else was a replacement for her.

Someone that Ryuto had truly cared about.

It was probably Tohko's mother, Yui.

The woman who had been Ryuto's first love.

"Everyone tosses me aside in the end. Yui's the only one who ever loved me. Yui gave me everythin'…kind words, warmth, all of it. And yet because Jerome cared for Alissa, Juliette couldn't help but get hurt and broken. If I were Jerome, I woulda loved Juliette. I woulda made Juliette happy."

A chill went through my heart.

When Ryuto had talked about Juliette before, I hadn't known whom he meant by "Juliette marrying Jerome."

But now that I knew Fumiharu was Jerome, Kanako was Alissa, and Yui was Juliette, Ryuto's words became cloaked in a different meaning.

Jerome loved Alissa and didn't love Juliette.

Which meant Fumiharu Amano loved Kanako Sakurai and wasn't in love with Yui Amano—

It was as if a pitch-black shadow had fallen over me; I could barely breathe, and I quickly denied the thoughts rising in my heart.

I didn't want to think that the memories of her parents that Tohko had recounted so joyfully were a lie.

Her voice kind, as if a tender past had risen in the back of her mind. Sweet yearning coloring her eyes.

*"When my dad proposed to my mom, he said, 'I want you to be my author. Just mine.' My dad and I both loved the meals my mom wrote for us."*

The photo of her parents that I'd found in Tohko's room had looked happy, too.

But immediately after denying this, doubts bubbled up once more.

How my literary agent Mr. Sasaki had said Fumiharu and Kanako's relationship was a "chaste union."

And how he had said that maybe Fumiharu understood Kanako as an author better than anyone and also how Kanako had often done things to rub Yui's nose in her relationship with Fumiharu—

A shuddering chill crawled up my spine.

As I wavered, Ryuto whispered the seeds of a fresh doubt into my ear with his humid breath.

"Juliette was such a truly kind woman. She couldn't take it forever, the way Jerome had eyes only for Alissa…In order to have Jerome all for herself, she poisoned him."

Maybe he was worn out from crying, but he didn't wail the way he had been. Instead, he whispered in a low, rough voice, almost a pant. It was pretty unsettling, and I had the impression that poison was being dripped into my ear, drop by drop.

*Drip…drip…*

"Konoha…Juliette kept the violet, heart-shaped bottle full of poison in a drawer of her dressin' table in her bedroom. She put it in her jewelry box and locked it.

"Takin' it out when no one else was around, she would gaze at it, entranced—and one day she mixed it into the coffee she and Jerome were gonna drink."

Reality was probably getting mixed up with fantasy because he was drunk. He described the scene back then as if speaking in a dream.

"She stuck a spoon into the coffeepot and swirled it around… and the silver dust spun in a smooth circle, dissolvin' into it.

"Yui's hands were pale and silky—the sleeve of her sweater ended in a bloodred cuff, and the poison cascaded down from it…

"Spilling…spilling…shining silver sand…

"Yui watched it with a soft smile. Now I won't have to suffer. I'll be able to sleep in peace…Her face joyful with that thought… When I tried to help her put it in the cups, she told me I was too little and I might hurt myself. Then she picked up the coffeepot and poured it into some cups with flowers on them. That's when the earth cracked open and turned dark.

"Every day…I have the same dream…every day.

"I dream that I give Yui the bottle.

"I dream that I die alone in a hospital.

"And then someone points at a shelf—"

Ryuto lifted his face and pointed unsteadily toward the top of the wall.

"—and they tell me. The sleepin' powder of Ole Lukøje is up there—"

I gulped at the dangerous look in his eyes, as if he was possessed by something—as if he was seeing a vision.

But it didn't feel right.

"I thought the heart-shaped bottle was shut inside a drawer in her dressing table? That's what you said before."

"That's true . . . I wonder why that is."

Confusion came over Ryuto's face. But his eyes immediately turned dark and dangerous again, as if he'd slipped back inside himself, and his gaze fell to the carpet. With a frightened expression he murmured, "I'm positive . . . it's gonna happen again. If I . . . have a kid with Maki, it's gonna be a boy."

The air grew thick and murky. I could feel my skin humming and the dryness in my throat. His head still bowed, Ryuto shook it side to side.

"No . . . if I don't cut this off somehow . . . there's no meaning in getting reborn . . ."

No . . . *no* . . .

I listened to the words Ryuto continued to groan in a low voice, as if listening to an ominous prophesy, my body growing cold and stiff.

Even after Ryuto fell asleep, his voice lingered in my mind.

No . . . *no* . . .

———⟫◆⟪———

Happiness as an author—I wonder what that is.

Last night I reread *Strait Is the Gate*.

Something more important than happiness—Alissa's answer was sanctity.

I wonder why she had to go so far in turning her back on Jerome when she did love him.

The stories you make with Fumiharu are more and more luminous and you're getting closer to the supreme story.

No matter how repulsive the thing you write about, there's no immediacy. It stabs straight into the reader's heart and excites a transparent ache.

But I feel as though the more you write, the more alone you become, and I worry.

I get so uneasy I can't stand it, like Juliette who could do nothing but stand by and watch as Alissa went through the narrow gate.

In my head, I understand that going down that path is the right thing for you, Kana, but my heart is practically being torn apart.

I'm practically screaming at you, with all the strength in my voice, "Don't go that way! Don't go through the gate! Please, come back!"

I was the one who brought you and Fumiharu together.

Fumiharu read an essay you had in our club magazine and said he wanted to meet you.

The first time all three of us ate out together, you barely spoke and you glowered at Fumiharu, so I was on pins and needles.

I knew you were shy in front of strangers, so I thought you wouldn't really want to meet Fumiharu, either. And yet when I said, "Do you want to get something to eat, the three of us?" you agreed without any fuss, so I was relieved.

And then you were sullen as soon as we sat down, so my stomach was really tight and I could hardly taste the food.

Though it didn't look like Fumiharu was worried about it. He was smiling placidly.

"She's a lovely woman. And extremely intelligent to boot."

When he complimented you afterward—"Isn't she?!"—my voice rose accidentally.

I was thrilled that Fumiharu was taken with my best friend, whom I was so proud of.

I never thought he would contact you...

That he would have you write that novel.

That the two of you were meeting up in secret.


I became Fumiharu's wife, and you, Kana, became an author.


Was that truly the best thing for you, Kana?

Fumiharu gently admonished that pestering you about all this would only interfere with you.

It was the same with Takumi.

He said you could make decisions for yourself, so I shouldn't meddle...

But...

## Chapter 3—Words Hidden

Ryuto's assault ended and days went by in peace.

When I asked Takeda after school in the library how he was doing, she told me with a distant expression, "He's drowning in the dumps.

"He went to see Himekura again yesterday, and I guess she chased him off."

"...Are you mad?"

"No, not at all."

"I think Ryuto wants you to comfort him."

"If you spoil him, you get into the habit of doing it, so I'm going to let him be depressed awhile. That makes things more peaceful for you guys, too, right?"

"That's true..."

My voice choked off.

"Takeda... what will you do if Maki has Ryuto's baby?"

"I'm not going to do anything. Ryu just isn't capable of going out with one girl, and I bet he'll have oodles of babies on the side later on. I can't let every single one of them bother me."

I felt a little sorry for Ryuto after all.

Takeda went back to the checkout desk, so while I waited for

Kotobuki, I walked around scanning the shelves for something to read.

My breath caught when I found *Strait Is the Gate*, and unconsciously I came to a stop.

My pulse quickened and something deep in my chest squeezed tight.

Beside it was a thin volume with the title *A Hidden Diary*. The author was Gide.

I'd been trying not to think about Tohko or the Amanos this whole time.

It was better not to get involved any further.

And yet my fingers stretched out hesitantly for the book again and again.

I took it down with a feeling of shame, as if I were doing something I shouldn't, and I turned back the drab green cover.

*"I was thinking about her last night. As I often do, I was having a discussion with her in my mind, more at my ease than when I stand before her in reality. But abruptly I said to myself, 'But she's dead…'"*

This…was a novel?

*"I won't deny that I have frequently lived at a distance from her for long periods. However, ever since my youth it has been my habit to report to her the conquests of the day and to share with her the sorrows and joys within my solitary breast. So I did again last night, but abruptly I recalled that she was dead."*

While I moved to a table to continue reading, I realized that it was a diary Gide had written in the style of a memoir about his wife, Madeleine. When I looked at the explanatory notes, they said the book had been published after his death.

Ryuto had said that Gide was a homosexual and that he'd had no marital relations with Madeleine. Had said he was awful for writing down anything and everything in his diaries and novels...But in his diary, Madeleine was the person Gide loved best and he had lamented her death.

*"Everything has faded and lost its luster."*

*"Because I have lost her, I have no reason to live. I no longer know for what reason I would go on living hereafter."*

Sadness that dug at my chest. Despair. The shriek of a soul that could not set aside its pen—each word that Gide wrote racked my heart.

He recorded how he had made Madeleine the point of departure for Alissa in *Strait Is the Gate*, but that she was not Madeleine herself. She hadn't appeared to find anything of herself in it, and during her life, she never spoke a word about the book.

Still, as I read through the diary, I also realized that things that had actually happened to Gide and Madeleine had been liberally mixed into episodes between Alissa and Jerome.

The part where Alissa is hurt when she discovers her mother's unfaithfulness and Jerome promises to protect her for the rest of his life was identical, and Gide told a story similar to the scene with the cross in his diary. I felt as if Jerome's psychology in continuing to love Alissa as something saintly mirrored Gide's feelings, loving Madeleine for being immaculate.

*"I thought that if I drew closer to God, it would bring me that much closer to her. And while I did so, slowly ascending to heaven, I felt that the land around us was gradually narrowing. I was overjoyed."*

Even though he loved her that much, Gide was unable to see Madeleine as a sexual object.

That fact brought sorrow and discord into their relationship.

*"I've been so naive, I never even once considered whether or not love without physicality would satisfy her."*

*"I thought desire was the purview of men. It was more reassuring to think that women were incapable of experiencing that sort of desire; that even if they could, it was only 'women of the evening.'"*

Gide's excuse was selfish. I wondered how Madeleine must have felt as a wife whose husband never sought physical relations from her.

Plus, in the notes it said that it wasn't even as if Gide only had sexual intercourse with men; he had a child with a girl who was young enough to be his daughter.

So then why was Madeleine the only one he'd been unable to sleep with? Was it because Madeleine had such a saintly role for him?

From an old photograph, Madeleine spoke to Gide, who was sunk into melancholy. She told him, *"My greatest joys are thanks to you."*

*"And my greatest sorrows, as well. So both the best and the most painful."*

The relationship was suffering as well as joy for both of them—even when he was away from her, Gide sent Madeleine letters. For him, they were special letters. He wrote down "the best of himself" in his letters. His spirit, his joys, changes in his mood, the work of the day: everything.

But after Gide left on a trip with a man who was his lover, Madeleine burned all the letters he had sent her.

Gide took such a shock from that act that it almost drove him insane, and he slipped into despondency, saying, *"The best parts of myself have been eradicated."*

But Madeleine experienced such pain that she could do nothing else. She appealed to him.

*"They were the most important things in the world to me."*

*"After you left, I knew not what I ought to do nor what would become of me in this huge house you had abandoned, with no one in it I might rely upon. At my most desolate moment...for the first time I thought there was nothing for me but to die."*

*"I truly suffered...I burned your letters in order to do something. Before I did it, I read them all over again, one by one..."*

Their feelings gradually drifted apart and the diary grew thick with words of suffering.

He suffered when he was with her, but he couldn't leave her; he was in love—as I turned the pages, my throat tightened and grew hot at the suffocating conflict.

Maybe if Gide had been able to love Madeleine physically, too, their relationship might have become something different.

Maybe Gide would have been able to build a peaceful, serene household with Madeleine, without having affairs or so often vacating the house to travel.

Following Madeleine's death, Gide's psyche deteriorated rapidly.

*"After her passing, I am only playing at being alive."*

*  *  *

It had been Madeleine after all who'd been the wellspring of creativity for Gide, and she'd had a special role that was etched into his soul.

I was sucked in by their mad, eerie love to the point it made my skin thrum. And as it was happening, Kanako and Fumiharu came to mind. Kanako who'd said that their relationship was a "chaste union."

Maybe Kanako and Fumiharu had been deeply linked by some other element than physical desire between a man and a woman, the way Gide and Madeleine had been.

And maybe Fumiharu's wife, Yui, had suspected...

The image of Madeleine burning the letters overlaid itself on Yui.

How had Yui felt as she waited for Fumiharu, who was so often out of the house for his work as an editor?

I had sunk so deeply into thoughts so bleak it felt wrong to touch them any further that I hadn't noticed that Kotobuki was there.

"Sorry to keep you waiting, Inoue... Inoue?"

"Er, oh! You're closing already?"

I quickly shut the book and stood up. I returned it to the shelf, hiding the title and author's name.

"Let's head out then."

Her white scarf wrapped around her, Kotobuki had been looking at me with concern, but she nodded okay and took my hand.

We walked down the dim streets hand in hand.

Talking about maybe going somewhere since tomorrow was Saturday.

"There's a movie I want to see."

"Which one?"

"Well... don't laugh."

Kotobuki's cheeks flushed red, and then in a quiet voice, she told me the title of a romantic movie starring a female pop star.

"That's cool. Let's do that."

"R-really? If you don't want to, I can go see it with Mori and them. It's fine."

"You want to see it, though, right?"

"Y-yeah."

"Then I want to see it, too."

Kotobuki's face bloomed into an excited smile. The ends of her white scarf swayed.

"Thanks, Inoue."

"You should come to my house afterward."

"Wha—?"

Kotobuki's eyes widened, and embarrassed, I explained. "I promised I would introduce you to my parents for real. As my girlfriend."

"Uh…I, uh…"

"Do you have other plans?"

Kotobuki shook her head pertly.

"No. Oh, but…"

Her face clouded slightly.

"If we're seeing the movie first, I guess I can't bring any lemon meringue pie…"

I laughed.

"You could do that next time. Or you could bake it in our kitchen if you wanted."

"Oh…I wouldn't feel right doing that yet."

She fluttered her free hand in nervous dismissal. Then she tightened the hand that held mine.

"N-next time…okay?"

"Can't wait."

I looked her in the eyes when I said it, and she lowered them with a shy, excited expression.

"I'll make some cookies instead. Something not too sweet. Right now I'm thinking salt cookies, maybe..."

As soon as she said it, she looked surprised and choked off the rest.

When I saw that, I realized what Kotobuki must have associated the salt cookies with.

The sharply sweet taste of the cream puffs reawoke on my tongue.

"Uh, I-I could also do cocoa flavored or ones with black tea leaves in them, or—"

Kotobuki was speaking quickly, desperately.

I pretended not to notice and murmured, "That sounds good."

I was sure we were both thinking of the same person right then.

I felt as if my emotions would overflow when I saw the white scarf around Kotobuki's throat. When I averted my gaze, something was fluttering in the spot where my eyes landed.

Something thinner and wispier than the scarf...A white ribbon tangled around the branch of a tree that jutted out over the wall of someone's home. It looked like the ribbon from a school uniform, and my eyes widened.

"...Inoue, what's wrong?"

"There's a ribbon up there."

"What? No. That's a strip of plastic."

"...So it is."

Why had I thought it was a ribbon?

"Speaking of which, did you know that if you tie a ribbon to a tree at school, your wish will come true?"

My heart skipped a beat at Kotobuki's question.

A scene rose in my mind's eye.

A bright, sunny sky after a spring shower.

A tall tree thick with green leaves.

Tohko desperately scrambling up it.

They said that if you tied a ribbon to a tree at school without anyone seeing you, your wish would come true.

It was a trick with absolutely no scientific basis that girls seemed to love.

Tohko must have been giving it a shot herself. She'd untied the turquoise ribbon on her chest, and just at the point that she was tying it around a branch, her hand slipped and she almost tumbled out of the tree. I'd rushed over to her, and the ribbon that had slipped from her hand fluttered down right in front of me.

Tohko had turned bright red at having her underclassman witness her in such a pathetic state.

*"Ack! Why are you here?!"*

*"I came to school early because I've got hall monitor duty. What were you doing?"*

*"What?! Uh...a baby bird fell out of its nest, so I was putting it back!"*

Making up excuses, she climbed down, tears in her eyes as she told me, *"Don't look up my skirt."*

"If someone sees you, it doesn't work. That's a lot harder than it sounds."

"Oh...yeah, it is."

"Have you ever tied up a ribbon, Inoue?"

"Wha—? No, uh, I don't really..."

"R-right. Magic tricks are so childish, right?" Kotobuki said, flustered.

My heart was racing almost painfully. Melancholy and guilt that seemed to stab at my heart spread out from within my body.

When she saw my face stiffening, her expression grew fragile. I saw it happening and squeezed Kotobuki's hand tightly again and smiled.

"What time should we see the movie? Earlier is better probably."

"Y-yeah."

Strength came into Kotobuki's fingertips, too. She squeezed my hand firmly, as if injecting it with her determination to never let go. But instead it seemed to reveal her uneasy state of mind.

The wind grew a little cooler. Her white scarf fluttered.

As each of us pretended not to notice the other's anxiety, we went on talking in cheerful voices.

I walked Kotobuki home; promised, "I'll call you later," with a smile; and then left.

I had reached my limit. The instant I was alone, the darkness enveloping my body increased its hold. I could no longer ignore the heartbreak that constricted my chest.

I hadn't seen Tohko for several days now.

I hadn't heard her voice, either.

I was trying to forget about her, but I couldn't. She was always present deep inside my heart, and she reappeared on me like this at the slightest provocation.

My throat grew hot and my chest hurt, as if it were about to rip apart.

I'd managed to put the memory of Miu, whom I'd loved so much, behind me.

At some point I would be okay.

A time would come when I could forget about Tohko.

A time when her image would be hazy even if I played it over, like an old and broken videotape—a time when I would be able to accept that fact with only a tiny bit of sadness—I knew that day would come.

All I needed to do was wait for the time to pass.

Forgetting the pain and sadness: that was the most effective way. There wasn't anything I *could* do but that...

The wind grew even stronger. The ends of my hair hit my cheeks.

I bit down on my lip and bowed my head, then followed the dark road feeling gloomy.


On Saturday morning, the sky was a little cloudy.

I checked the chance of rain on the Internet, then put a collapsible umbrella in my bag and got myself ready.

I'd told my mom the night before that Kotobuki was coming over after the movie.


"We're going to eat lunch here. Would you mind making it for us? That and dessert. Something a girl would like this time."

"Kotobuki is the girl who went home so early last time, isn't she? You know, your mother has been giving this a lot of thought, and I have to ask: Are you, Kotobuki, and Ryuto in a love triangle? I was so sure you and Amano..."

My mom came out with something Mori might have said. I flatly denied it.

"No, we are not. Ryuto has his own girlfriends, and Tohko... is just my club president. I'll reintroduce Kotobuki the right way tomorrow. Get Dad to be here, too."

My mom wore a complicated expression.


At noon my mom asked me if a paella and strawberry Bavarian cream would be all right.

"Yeah, thanks. I think she'll like that," I answered, then left the house early.

The wind pricked at my skin. It was already March, but apparently spring was still a little ways off.

The news even said that the cherry blossoms would be early this year.

As I walked, I opened my cell phone and sent Kotobuki a text.

Morning. I just left.

That was when my phone rang with an incoming call.

I jumped at the solemn, oppressive tune that reminded me of a Mass and my heart shrank in on itself.

I looked at the name displayed on the screen, and a chill went through my spine.

Ryuto!

Why was he calling now? I hadn't heard a word from him ever since he'd gotten so stinking drunk and weepy at my house.

A chill crawled up from my feet. Was he planning to do something again?

"Hello?"

When I answered clumsily, I heard sniffling.

"Konoha, you gotta help me."

"What's going on, Ryuto?"

My pulse quickened at his peculiar manner. It sounded like he was crying.

"Tohko's—"

"What about Tohko?!"

"You gotta help. I can't do it. You gotta come here right away. If you don't, Tohko's gonna disappear! It's gotta be you. I mean, you're Tohko's—I'm beggin' ya. You gotta help Tohko."

The call ended there.

What had happened to Tohko?!

Blood rushed up to my head, and the skin prickled all over my body.

*Calm down; this could be another of Ryuto's traps.* The same thing had happened before. He lied and told me that Tohko had been poisoned and made me go see her.

But his tone was more desperate than last time, and his repeated begging, "Please, please," had been in a voice wet with tears.

Besides, even that other time, Tohko might not have been poisoned, but she'd had a terrible fever, which had left her bedridden. If I hadn't gone, she might have suffered all alone in her frigid house.

Bitter saliva built up inside my mouth.

I was so conflicted over whether I should go to Tohko or whether I should continue on my way to the place I was meeting Kotobuki that my vision blurred.

If this was a trap set by Ryuto, Kotobuki might be in danger.

I recalled what he'd done in the basement storage room, and my brain flared with rage. I wasn't going to let him act like that ever again with Kotobuki. I wouldn't let him lay a finger on her. I'd decided to protect her.

But if Ryuto was truly looking for my help—if something had happened to Tohko—

I broke out in a sweat as a variety of scenarios tumbled through my mind.

With trembling fingers, I called Kotobuki's cell phone.

A message played saying it was unable to connect, maybe because she'd left her house, too. What should I do?! It would have been perfect if I could have torn myself in two and gone two different places. But that wasn't possible.

My vision blurred even further, and my head felt like it was going to split open.

What should I do? What should I—

In a daze, with a sheet of sweat on my fingers, I dialed Akutaga-wa's number.

"What's wrong, Inoue?"

The instant I heard his honest voice, the blockades on my strained emotions shattered.

"I have a favor to ask, Akutagawa! I can't make it to the place I'm supposed to meet Kotobuki anymore. Could you go for me?"

I explained the situation quickly, my throat aching as if I was being strangled, unable to breathe, and my chest threatening to rip apart.

My feet were already carrying me to Tohko. That fact became a wave of pitch-black despair and crashed over me.

I'd sworn that I would protect Kotobuki. And yet, in my ears a voice accused that when the time came, I'd chosen Tohko again. Each time I took another step forward, it was as if I were being struck by biting whips.

No! It wasn't true! I hadn't chosen Tohko!

But when I thought that I might never be able to see Tohko again, my body felt like it might tear itself to pieces. I couldn't bear it.

If Tohko really were to disappear—!

If she stopped existing in this world—!

No matter how I argued that there was no chance of something like that happening, I couldn't keep myself from going to her.

Because deep in my heart, I'd been thinking about Tohko this whole entire time. Because I missed her more than anything.

I couldn't stop my heart from going to her. The happy hours I'd spent with Kotobuki, the warm, ticklish conversations and smiles, the sensation of our hands intertwined had blown away in an instant!

My head filled with Tohko to the point of despair.

The way Gide had returned to Madeleine, no matter how many lovers he had—the way Madeleine had been the only person with whom he could share his honest feelings, no matter how far apart they were—

I, too, understood then that wherever I was, whoever I loved, whoever I belonged to, if anything happened to Tohko, I wouldn't be able to help but throw it all away and run to her.

In the midst of an extremity that would not allow retreat, Ryuto always prodded at me with merciless force—with merciless cruelty. Made me realize.

What Tohko's life was like!

That I would never be able to forget!

I didn't know if Ryuto had deliberately created this situation and forced me to choose. But if so, then you win!

The Sakurai home, which I was visiting for the third time, was wrapped in the brooding air of winter.

Even though I rang the bell repeatedly as white breath spilled from my mouth, there was no answer. And there was no sign that anyone was home. The blinds and curtains I could see from outside were all pulled shut.

Like the last time I'd come, the front door wasn't locked. I pulled it open without even announcing myself and called out, "Tohko!"

"Tohko! Tohko!"

I yelled until my throat was raw, but the book girl with her braids never appeared. And I never heard her bounding voice. The interior of the old house was eerily silent.

I yanked my shoes off and headed straight to Tohko's room. As soon as I slid her door open, my eyes landed on the scattered shreds of a uniform.

The heart-stopping shock sent my mind momentarily blank.

A carpet was laid in the center of the woven mat floor and scattered on top of it like torn-up paper were the sleeves, the collar, the skirt of a school uniform. Even the turquoise ribbon that fluttered against Tohko's chest had been torn in two and thrown aside. Beside it, much like a bouquet set beside a grave, was a basket holding a huge number of Casablanca lilies.

My chest tightened and I grew dizzy, and in the moment when I stumbled, I reached a hand out. It struck a bookshelf, scattering the books on the middle shelf across the woven mat floor.

The books collided with one another, striking my ears with a sharp sound.

A makeup box covered with pale violet rice paper tumbled from the shelf along with them. The lid came off and a huge number of letters spilled out. The pastel tones of the envelopes—rosy pink and sky blue and others—spread out in a fan at my feet.

I crouched down hurriedly and gathered them up with shaking hands and saw that every one of the envelopes was still sealed. On the front was an address and the name "Kanako Sakurai" and the return address was "Yui Amano."

Letters that Yui had sent to Kanako? Why this many? And none of them were open? Had Kanako refused to read them?

I couldn't reach a logical conclusion. Looking at the strange letters, my anxiety swelled even more. Where had Tohko gone?

My shoulders heaving as I breathed, I stacked the fallen books up on the floor, then returned the letters to the box, set it beside the books, and stood up.

"Tohko! Tohko!"

The shouts that flew from my convulsing throat were nearly a shriek.

I ran down the hall and opened every last one of the doors.

"Tohko! Where are you? Tohko!!"

A sloppy room that looked like it belonged to Ryuto. A room

with a woman's mirrored vanity table in it, the kitchen, the bathroom, the living room—Tohko was in none of them.

I called Ryuto on my cell phone. But he didn't pick up! The sweat that had broken out on my skin chilled, robbing my body of its heat. My head was burning hot.

It was when I was standing frozen, trembling, in the middle of the living room that I caught sight of a torn-up letter lying on the floor beside the table.

When I picked it up, I saw the message written on it.

*"Aunt Kanako:*

*"Welcome home. I hope you had a good day at work.*
*"The publisher mailed you a lot of boxes and papers, so I put them over there.*
*"Now I'm going to do as I've been planning and—"*

The rest had been torn away, so I didn't know what it said. I crawled around on the floor hunting for the rest of the letter, but I couldn't find it.

What had she planned?!

Ryuto still wasn't picking up his cell phone. But Kanako—she might know where Tohko was!

If I explained the situation to Mr. Sasaki, would he be able to tell me where Kanako's office was? Actually, the letter had said that packages had arrived from the publisher. There were papers and postcards and small packages sitting together in a pile on the table.

When I looked through their addresses, I found an invoice from a flower shop and a printed card among them. It looked like a thank-you note from someone who'd attended a seminar Kanako had appeared in, and it said they would be sending flowers. The recipient was Kanako, but the return address belonged to an apartment building in the city.

I remembered the bouquet of lilies in Tohko's room. Kanako might have had them delivered to her house since she couldn't take them at her office!

The recipient's phone number was noted on the invoice, and I called it without any hesitation. I was transferred to an answering machine and the introduction played.

*No one home—?* No, maybe they just weren't answering. I spoke quickly.

"This is Inoue, Tohko's underclassman. There's something very urgent I'd like to speak to Kanako Sakurai about, so if you're there, please pick up. Please."

I heard the sound of the receiver being picked up.

In a haze, I yelled, "Is this Kanako?!"

"...What do you want?"

Her voice was as cool as ice. My spine flashed cold, and I shrank in on myself in instinctive fear of someone who was unquestionably superior.

I swallowed thickly and then asked, "Do you know where Tohko went?"

"You called here to ask something so stupid?"

Her voice was tinged with irritation.

"I'm sorry, but it's extremely urgent."

"She went to be with Yui, if you must know."

The call cut off. Kanako had hung up.

What did that mean, to be with Yui? Yui was dead!

I tried calling back, but no matter how I yelled for her, Kanako didn't pick up.

It felt as if my body was caught in a hot wind, and it was hard to breathe.

I took the invoice with the address and phone number of her office on it and ran out of the house.

The apartment was on the same train line as the Sakurai house. With the walk, it took nearly an hour to get there, and then I climbed the stairs.

It was an old building showing its age and it didn't have an elevator.

Considering that after the murder-suicide of her parents, Kanako had gone on living in the same house, maybe she wasn't a fan of moving.

Or maybe she didn't much concern herself about where she lived. The room at the home that seemed to belong to her was frigid and had almost no furniture, either.

There was no nameplate posted on the corner room on the fifth floor. I stood in front of the door and rang the bell, but there was no answer. I rang it again and again, and finally the door opened.

Kanako appeared wearing a simple black knit top with a long black skirt, her eyes cold and piercing.

Even under these circumstances, seeing her up close, she was witheringly beautiful and frosty, as if clad in ice crystals.

"Why did you come here? I'm busy. Leave."

I stopped her from closing the door by putting my body inside the frame, and I begged, "Please tell me where Tohko went! There was a torn-up school uniform scattered around her room—but she wasn't there! I found a note addressed to you in the living room. That was torn up, too, so I could only read part of it. What was she planning to do?"

Kanako's response was cold.

"What will you do if you find out?"

"I'll go see her."

"You might not be able to, you know."

Her dark voice and empty eyes sent a shudder down my spine.

Even though I'd told her that Tohko's uniform had been ripped up, the woman wasn't concerned in the slightest. It seemed like she didn't care what happened to Tohko.

Utter indifference.

Rejection.

*This woman scares me.*

This woman, who declared without hesitation that being an author meant passing through the narrow gate alone, who had put that into practice and wrote down every detail of the deaths of her own parents and her own friends—she was scary.

This woman, who in her book calmly murdered the girl who lived in her house with her, the memento of her late friends; this woman, who could treat her as if she didn't exist—this woman, who lived as an author scared me. She was too unsettling to understand.

Just having her stare at me, my spine trembled uncontrollably and I wanted to flee.

Even so, I planted my feet and declared, "I'll go see her, even if I can't find her." Kanako turned her back on me and went into the apartment.

"Wait, please!"

I pulled my shoes off and pushed inside, too.

"If you know where Tohko went, please tell me."

Kanako didn't even turn around. The kitchen was right next to the front door, and her workroom was past that. There was a desktop computer on top of a big, broad desk. In front of it were scattered a bunch of photos showing roads, houses, gardens, school buildings, trees and fields, orchards, art museums, and stuff like that in the area. I suppose it was material for a novel.

Besides that, she also had a blue memo book and a silver pen, a flower-patterned teacup, a tart piled with strawberries, and cookies lined up on a white plate with a lace pattern around its edges, and there were several translucent purple spoon rests arrayed with a gold fork, spoon, and knife on them.

Was she having a one-person tea party?

"Please, Kanako. Her room wasn't the way it should be! When you said she's with Yui, where did you mean?! There were tons of letters from Yui addressed to you in Tohko's room. Does it have anything to do with that?!"

"Letters from Yui?"

Kanako had been acting uninterested until then, but suddenly her forehead wrinkled and her face grew harsh as she glared at me.

"What sort of letters?"

"They hadn't been opened, so I don't know. But if you know where Tohko is—"

When I said that, she grabbed the memo book and pen from her desk with an exasperated motion, wrote something down, then tore the page out and handed it to me.

When I accepted it and looked to see what she'd written, I saw an address. Iwate Prefecture? Is that where Tohko was?!

I was just about to thank her when Kanako murmured in a frigid voice that made me shudder, "That's the grave of someone who took poison and died out of weakness. I wish that girl wouldn't come back. But she will."

When I lifted my face, I met her fierce, hate-filled eyes. It was the first strong emotion Kanako had shown.

Eyes like fire, burning insanely—

78

Naked loathing—

My mouth dried out and a shiver ran down my spine.

So this woman could look like this, too.

Perhaps Arisa, the main character of *The Immoral Passage*, the book that had been modeled on the Amanos, had had these same terrifying eyes when she strangled the infant Toco. She looked possessed.

At that thought, my spine chilled even further. Somehow I forced out some words of gratitude, and I left her apartment.

⟫◈⟪

I don't understand, Kana.

The joy of being an author and the ordinary happiness of being a person.

Both should be important, but if you had to choose only one, which should I recommend that you choose?

Which do you desire?

Is a family superfluous to you, Kana? Are children and a life partner an unnecessary weight to you, Kana?

Do you hate it that much when little Ryu calls you mom? Is it that much of a hassle for you to smile when Tohko calls you Aunt Kanako?

Ryu and Tohko are both waiting for you to speak to them.

Even Takumi honestly cared about you. And yet when he died, you didn't even go to the hospital. And you worked through his funeral.

While Takumi was in surgery, as I carried Tohko in my arms, I prayed so hard for you to come for him that it almost crushed my heart.

At the funeral, I felt so bad for Takumi that I held Tohko in my arms, and yes, I wept.

Can you be happy continuing down that narrow path all alone? Are you content living as an author?

I had another fight with Fumiharu—even though tomorrow we have to go to a wedding—even though the children are sleeping in the next room.

"Fumiharu, you have a wife in me, a daughter in Tohko, and an author in Kana. You want for Kana to be alone, but you get the joy of having it both ways. You're not being fair!"

When I said that, Fumiharu smiled and said, "You're right. I'm not being fair."

His smile was incredibly clear, and gentle, and yet sad, and I couldn't attack him anymore.

I've looked at the little violet bottle Takumi gave me so many times.

———————◆———————

I took the bullet train to Sendai, then transferred from there to another line, then caught a taxi after that, so that it took nearly three hours for me to reach the temple whose name was written in the note.

The sky was a dark leaden color, and it felt colder than when snow was falling. The air seemed to cut at my skin and bite into my bones. There were fields and rice paddies on all sides, and the exposed earth was a dusty white and looked cold, too.

I'd underestimated winter in the north. As I regretted not buying disposable hand warmers at the train station, my teeth chattering, I went into a temple that looked like it might rot away at any moment.

"Hello?" I called out, and an aged head priest who looked like he was over ninety years old appeared.

I told him that I had come to see Tohko, and in a gentle north-eastern accent, he told me to try the graveyard in the back. That she would probably be there, if she hadn't already left.

Running with all my strength, the air scraped at my skin, prickling it. My heart swelled with anxiety over what I would do if she wasn't there and also with the anticipation of being able to see her in only a few more minutes. My heart was practically exploding.

When the graveyard came into view with its smoky black and gray gravestones, my pulse quickened all the more.

But no matter how hard I looked, I couldn't see anyone there.

I was too late—

Just as disappointment was making it difficult to breathe, a small head with dangling long braids bobbed up beyond a gravestone.

Apparently she'd stood up from a crouch. Her head was still bent, gazing at a grave...

The familiar profile...

The navy duffle coat...

The academy's uniform...

The black braids spilling over her shoulders...

My throat trembled and a hot lump rose up in it.

Bursting with emotions, I called out to her.

"Tohko...!"

Her braids wavered delicately as she looked at me, her eyes went round, and her face told me that she couldn't believe I was there.

I'd finally found her—

The mere fact of our gazes catching made my feelings ease, made the back of my throat swell, and I thought I might start crying.

It had been only a brief time that we were apart, but it felt as if we had gone such a long time without seeing each other. My heart fluttered.

I felt like if I looked away, Tohko would disappear. I was standing perfectly still, unable even to blink. Tohko was staring at me, not moving a muscle, either. From surprise to melancholy—I saw her expression change slowly, and my breath stopped in my chest.

Tohko's eyes were tearing up just like mine.

After the trembling silence had gone on—"Are you a raccoon sprite pretending to be Konoha?"—those were the words she ultimately spoke.

"Why would you say that?"

"Come on, it takes ten hours to get here from Tokyo."

"It doesn't take that long. It was only about four hours."

"No way."

"It's the truth. What did you do to make it take so long?"

"I took an overnight bus...and then..."

"You should have used the bullet train!"

I felt like collapsing on the spot.

What were we doing talking about this all the way out in Iwate Prefecture? Why was there no tension in this girl?

"Your uniform..."

"Hmm?"

"Never mind. It's nothing."

Ryuto had gotten me again. But the rage wouldn't come. The despair and terror I'd felt when I was yelling Tohko's name at Ryuto's house and desperately searching for her had melted away completely, and my heart was clearing, as if being bathed in light.

"Did you come to talk about uniforms?"

"I'm not that fixated on them."

"Then why are you here?"

Tohko closed her mouth, awaiting my answer. Her slightly upturned eyes were tinged as if she was ever so slightly afraid.

"Does it matter?" I asked and walked right up to her. "I just... felt like taking a trip."

Tohko's eyes grew slightly moist again.

"Who told you I was here? Ryuto?"

"It was Kanako."

"Aunt Kanako?"

She seemed surprised by my answer.

"She told you about this place? You went to see her? But she wasn't at home today, was she?"

"I...called her office. I found the number printed on an invoice. And then she told me the temple's address."

I was ashamed of muscling my way into her office of all places, and I couldn't tell Tohko what I'd done.

Tohko's eyes grew even wider; then her eyelids fell and her expression became peaceful.

"Oh...so Aunt Kanako told you where it was."

Her lips curved up and she looked happy.

*"Aunt Kanako is a good, kind person."*

Why did Tohko cling to Kanako so devotedly? It wasn't like Kanako tried to hide her loathing of Tohko.

Tohko did it despite the fact that Kanako had told me, "I wish that girl wouldn't come back."

Seeing Tohko sink her grip into the faintest happiness, my heart wrung tight.

"...Today was the anniversary of your parents' death, huh?"

Quietly, Tohko whispered, "...Yes."

She went to be with Yui...so this is what she'd meant. The

grave carved with the Amanos' names was beautifully clean and laid with white flowers.

"I read Kanako's novel."

Her slender shoulders trembled ever so slightly. She lifted her lowered lashes and looked at me. It was an unsurprised look, a calm, melancholy look that accepted the burden of sorrow.

"The stuff in *Immoral Passage* was about Kanako and your parents, wasn't it?"

Tohko lowered her gaze again and turned back to face the grave.

"...It's a novel. After all, Aunt Kanako wasn't there that morning nine years ago."

In the bone-cracking cold, I perked my ears up to listen to what Tohko said.

"That morning...my mom and my dad were going to a wedding, so they were all dressed up. My mom was wearing a light violet dress and the lace chiffon on it rustled...It was very pretty. But she was a little deflated and spaced out.

"I guess the night before, she'd had a fight with my dad...I was in bed in the room next door. I heard their voices and it woke me up. But I was scared, so I squeezed my eyes shut and pretended to be asleep.

"My dad was wearing a black suit and a white necktie.

"His face was gentle like always, and he brushed my bangs aside with his fingers and smiled at me and said, 'Good morning.'

"Ryuto told my mom, 'You're so pretty, Aunt Yui,' and he was clinging to her. That cheered my mom up and she smiled, too.

"It was all exactly like normal..."

Tohko's head drooped.

"My dad and I ate the 'breakfast' my mom wrote for us, Ryuto and my mom ate their regular food, and my dad made some coffee...and he drank it with my mom."

*　*　*

*Coffee?*

Something tugged at me. Maybe because I'd listened to Ryuto's almost delirious rambling. Juliette had put poison in the coffee…

"Your dad ate books, didn't he? And he drank coffee anyway?"

"Sometimes…he would drink it with my mom to keep her company. My mom preferred tea, but she had coffee in the mornings. She said it cleared her mind and woke her up."

Tohko's tone of voice had a little awkwardness to it. Her words were somber, and she made a slight motion with her right hand partway through, as if she were squeezing a small object. Her gaze stayed off to one side, gazing painfully at the lower part of the gravestone.

The rest was exactly as I'd heard from Mr. Sasaki and Maki. Tohko and Ryuto were left at the Sakurai household, and while Fumiharu and Yui were headed to the ceremony in their car, there was an accident and they were killed.

"My mom hugged me and told me to be a good girl and wait at Aunt Kanako's house. She told me not to misbehave for her…"

The final promise she'd made with her mother nine years ago.

Was Tohko keeping it even now?

Getting better on her own when she caught a cold, always smiling brightly in front of Kanako, so she wouldn't cause her any trouble…

How had Tohko felt when she was eight years old, waiting for her parents who never came home?

I pictured a little girl with braids, trembling from fear of ghosts in the house of a murder-suicide, and my chest creaked with pain.

"Ryuto said that…Kanako is like Alissa from *Strait Is the Gate*."

Tohko lifted her face and gave a fragile smile.

86

"It's true. Noble-minded, solitary…her eyes fixed on a place far away, not on this earth."

And then in her clear voice she told the story of *Strait Is the Gate*.

"Gide's *Strait Is the Gate* tastes like amber-colored consommé.

"Do you know how they make consommé, Konoha? You put meat, bones, vegetables, and seasonings into a giant pot; let it bubble gently for a couple hours over a low heat; then extract the bouillon that's turned into soup stock. Then you put the ingredients and some egg whites back into the bouillon…and you boil it. Then the impurities that bind to the egg whites rise to the top, and you skim them out carefully again and again. Finally, you pour it through a filter to take out the fat, and then at last the transparent soup is done.

"It's a recipe that takes a lot of work.

"At first sight, it looks simple and clear, but…it's hard to name all the things that went into it. Just like people's hearts, all sorts of feelings are mixed up and melt together…pure, like the warm golden light before evening…It has a melancholy taste…"

The book club where Tohko and I had spent our time after school came to mind.

The western sun shining in the window.

The tiny room filled with gentle, golden light. Tohko's clear voice floating through it. The sound of a mechanical pencil sliding over lined paper. Tohko peeking at it excitedly.

A time of happiness.

If I had to put into words the things I'd felt then, I would never be able to express them fully.

Too many different feelings were mixed together and yet pure—gentle, melancholy…

Under the leaden sky, in the frigid, almost frozen air, Tohko went on talking.

87

There was no one among the crowd of gravestones but me and Tohko. It was as if we were standing all alone in another world, cut off from the reality outside.

Tohko's eyes were looking into the distance, wavering desolately.

"Jerome loved Alissa.

"And Alissa cared about Jerome. She also prayed that her younger sister Juliette would be happy.

"And Juliette did the same...Even as she loved Jerome, she hoped that he and Alissa would get married and be happy.

"Everyone was being more considerate of the others than of themselves. So then why couldn't any of them be happy? Did they all have to go through the narrow gate?"

I wondered if she was remembering her father and mother as she talked about *Strait Is the Gate*.

The last part of what she said seemed to be speaking not about Alissa or Jerome, but Fumiharu, Yui, and Kanako.

Why did every one of them need to go through the narrow gate?

I doubted Tohko would come up with an answer, either.

She closed her mouth and was silent.

Gazing at the distant, leaden sky, as if praying for the miracle that would change the world...

I was right at her side, looking at her, and I, too, was filled with frustration and melancholy.

My chest ached.

A stinging pain.

Tohko sneezed softly.

"I'm sorry, I don't have a scarf or gloves today."

My scarf...I had given it to Kotobuki.

"It's okay."

Tohko smiled gently.

A pretty, fleeting smile that seemed ready to melt into the sad scenery.

An ache shot through my chest again, and I took gentle hold of Tohko's hand.

Her frozen hand trembled slightly.

Even so, as if partaking of each other's warmth, Tohko and I clasped our hands in silence. Simply quiet, our words locked in our hearts...

There was nothing else we could do in that moment. Just hold hands.

Even so, we couldn't stay here forever.

"...Let's go somewhere else. You can't catch cold."

"...You're right."

Tohko gazed sadly at the grave—perhaps she was giving her mother and father a final word. A moment later, after closing her eyes, she lifted her head and began to walk.

Our hands were still intertwined. Not tightly locked, but gently, enfolding...

"What are you going to do now?"

"There's somewhere I've been wanting to go."

"Can I go with you?"

After some hesitation, a look of impermanence in her eyes, she whispered, "...Okay."

## Chapter 4—A Dwindling Back, Not Even a Footfall

Tohko argued for taking a bus that ran only once every hour, but I convinced her to take a taxi. The place we were headed was a tiny hospital.

It probably also served as someone's house. The three-story hospital and a one-story house stood in the grounds enclosed by a low fence. There was a sign that read INTERNAL MEDICINE, OBSTETRICS, GYNECOLOGY.

"I was born here."

Tohko's eyes narrowed with a deeply emotional smile. Now that she mentioned it, I recalled that the musical birthday card in the closet had been sent by a hospital.

"Is this the first time you've come back?"

"Yes."

"But you've visited your parents' grave a bunch of times, right? How come you never once came here?"

At that, Tohko got a conflicted look on her face, and then she smiled ambiguously.

"...I was in a hurry."

I had a feeling it wasn't just that, but I couldn't ask her about it.

"It would be nice if the doctor remembered me."

"You were a baby, right? Your face and body have all changed. There's no way."

"But this doctor delivered my father and grandfather, too."

"How old is this doctor?!"

As we were talking in front of the sign, a middle-aged, heavy-set nurse came out.

"Oh—can I help you?"

Tohko, who was never timid with anyone, faltered uncharacteristically.

"Um, I-I was born at this hospital. I wanted to say hello to the doctor."

"You're in high school, aren't you? How old are you?"

"I'm a third-year in high school. I'll be eighteen soon."

The nurse frowned sadly.

"Then you won't want Mamoru. It'll be his grandfather, Kiichi. I'm very sorry, but the doctor passed away last year."

Tohko's face fell visibly.

"Oh…"

"I'm so sorry, after you've come all this way. If you don't mind, may I ask your name?"

"My name is Tohko Amano."

At that, the nurse's face shone.

"Why, little Tohko! Tohko after *Legends of Tono*, wasn't it?"

Tohko's cheeks flushed with happiness, too.

"That's right."

"I knew it! Ah, now that I know that, you look just like your mother. You really do take after her in the nose and around the eyes. I assisted at your birth."

The nurse who introduced herself as Ms. Hayashi invited us inside and even told us that the room where Tohko's mother had stayed was open right now, and she let us see it.

91

In the small private room on the third floor, we could look out over a rolling landscape from the window next to the bed.

"Your mother's name was Yui, wasn't it? She would often look out this window. You said your father was an editor? He was busy with his work just then and wasn't able to come visit her. Your mother must have been uneasy, having to give birth all alone in a strange place. Her face seemed so sad…It looked like she was worrying over something. Even so, she kept her spirits up and never uttered a word of complaint.

"The first time she held you in her arms, she smiled so happily!

"She pressed her face to your cheek and called your name— 'Tohko'—in a gentle voice. She said she'd taken it from *Legends of Tono*. Apparently they'd decided to call you Tohko if you were a girl. Your mother truly seemed so happy. She was overjoyed at your birth with all her heart. And now here you are, all grown up."

Tohko listened to Ms. Hayashi's story excitedly, her lips curved in a smile.

As if she were listening to a beautiful symphony.

⟹◆⟸

**To be honest, I've been jealous of your ties with Fumiharu, Kana.**

**Because when Fumiharu proposed to me, he said something to me.**

**He told me, "The stories you write are like home-cooked meals.**

**"Simple and warm and soothing to the spirit, but the flavor is too weak to market them; I don't think you could be an author for everyone.**

"But you can be my author. I love you and the things that you write. So please, be my author. Just mine."

And then, right in front of my eyes, he ate a piece of paper I had just written on.

I was able to become a wife for Fumiharu, but I couldn't become an author for the editor Fumiharu Amano. Fumiharu was kind enough to call me his author, but that's because his author is really you, Kana.

That hurts—

While Tohko was inside me, I was very nervous and tense— worrying that when Fumiharu didn't come home he might be with you.

That the two of you would go somewhere far away that I wasn't able to go while I was waiting perfectly alone in my room.

My world crumbled bit by bit from within, and one day it went completely dark.

Why don't you come home, Fumiharu?

You promised we would go shopping for things for the baby on Sunday, so why did you go off to work when Kana called you? Yesterday you were talking about naming the baby Tohko after *Legends of Tono* if it was a girl, and you had such a gentle look on your face, so why?

Why—why did you go to Kana again?

Pained, suffocating, feeling as if I was slowly sinking into darkness, irrevocably—Tohko was the one who saved me from that hell.

When I held the small, soft, freshly born life in my arms, I was enveloped in such happiness as I had never felt until then and I smiled.

She was so precious to me that I cried. I was so thrilled.
I was happy.

* * *

**But my joy made you miserable.**

———⟫◆⟪———

"My dad is from Iwate, which is the setting for *Legends of Tono*."

As we walked side by side down a raised path between the rice fields, dyed by the sunset, Tohko told me about it with a gentle face.

"The legends told through the years in this place were collected into a book like fairy tales.

"In *Legends of Tono*, a lot of goblins and benevolent spirits appear...like water-dwelling ghouls or bird-winged warriors with long noses...benevolent, childlike imps watching over houses...creatures unlike humans, who lived in the same land as humans, interacting with them. But you know what? There aren't any stories about a creature who gobbles up books."

She whispered in a quiet voice, her emotion plain and her eyes softly luminous.

"My father, and his father before him...and his father... back and back for ages, they all ate stories to stay alive. No one told of what to call a creature like that, so I don't know. So that's why—"

Tohko's steps came to a halt, and she turned her face in my direction, catching me by surprise.

And then she puffed her chest out cheerfully.

"I am simply a high school girl and, as you can see, a book girl!"

I know that her voice making that upbeat declaration and her shining smile were both things that Tohko had won through the years she'd lived.

I knew how many meanings were packed into the name book girl.

*"I am **not** a goblin! I'm just a book girl."*

*"I am a book girl who loves books so much that I want to devour them."*

That it was a life different from most people's. That fact had probably hurt her and caused her worry. Even so, she was wearing a brilliant smile. She pouted and sulked. *"I'm not a goblin."* She turned the pages of a book and talked exuberantly about it.

My chest grew hot at her radiant smile.

I was sorry for being mean and calling her a goblin...If I said that, I knew Tohko would just puff out her flat-as-a-board chest even more and laugh. *"As long as you get it now."*

So I walked beside her in silence.

We caught a taxi to the train station, and yet again I had to convince Tohko.

"A bus is fine. Let's do that."

"That's an overnight trip, though! It doesn't leave for a long, **long** time! We'd get there tomorrow morning!"

"But it's cheaper than the bullet train."

"Time is just as important as money. You're studying for your exams, right? You shouldn't be sparing one minute or even one second."

"That's true...but I don't have the money to go back on the bullet train."

Obviously I wasn't going to cast her off by telling her to take the bus by herself, so I wound up saying, "...I'll pay."

"What? No way!"

"I want to. Don't say a word."

"Th-then...let's at least connect on a local train and—"

"Service is going to stop partway today."

As Tohko dithered again, I groaned.

"It's an early birthday present."

Tohko's eyes popped.

"You remembered my birthday?"

"...It's March fifteenth, right? You forced me to buy a present for you half a year late. I'm not going to forget that."

I said it bluntly and her cheeks turned red.

When I saw that, I got embarrassed and turned my back on her.

"So we can take the bullet train home, right?"

"Konoha...," Tohko whispered. "I can walk home. So buy me books with my share."

I toyed with the idea of letting her jog home by herself.

Even after we were on the train, Tohko seemed rueful and kept saying things like, "Let's not transfer to the bullet train; we could stay on this one and take the local train as far as we can," or "If we hitchhiked from here, would you buy me a book with the money we save?"

"You have exams to take. Why don't you memorize some math formulas or something?"

"It's fine. There's no math on the second-round tests."

"If you take it too lightly, you're going to fail."

"Agggh! Don't say I'm going to fail or slip up or any of that!"

So she was worrying about it a little, evidently.

Outside the window, the sun had gone down and it was now pitch-black. There was no one in the train car but me and Tohko.

Sitting on the opposite side of the box seat, oblivious, Tohko looked out the window and murmured, "But...the overnight bus is romantic and wonderful, too. The only light comes from the emergency lighting in the floor, and lights stream by outside the window. It's like you're driving through the stars."

"Like in *Night of the Milky Way Railway*?"

As soon as I said it, I remembered that night at the planetarium. I got an image of my spirit suddenly separating from my body and flying through the night.

The domed sky.

The starry expanse Miyazawa had seen twinkling on all sides.

Tohko telling the story of Giovanni and Campanella in a clear voice.

*"Let's go together, Campanella."*

Had Giovanni and the others gazed at the rushing stars from the window of their train, too?

Tohko was still looking out the window. Her somber face was reflected in the scenery passing by.

My heart squeezed tight.

"...I wonder where Campanella went after that, all alone?"

Giovanni was left behind, and Campanella left him.

It resembled Jerome and Alissa.

The one who made the decision was always the one who left. No matter how much the one left behind cries and begs, it accomplishes nothing.

Had Tohko connected Alissa and Campanella, too? In a gloomy voice, she whispered, "Yeah. Maybe Campanella went through the narrow gate..."

The gentle vibration...*rattle-rattle*-ing...came up through my feet. It was very quiet inside the car.

Neither of us spoke.

What was Tohko thinking about?

She'd been able to talk lightly before, like she used to, but would she get awkward again when we reached Tokyo? But this time we'd never see each other again?

After we'd both slipped into silence, Tohko said abruptly, "I'm…hungry."

"I haven't had anything since breakfast, either. Try to ignore it."

"But I'm so hungry I can't even believe it."

Her face fell and she looked like she was about to cry.

But actually, it would be kind of problematic if I wrote an improv story and she crunched it up right here. Even though, unlike the overnight bus, there weren't any other passengers around. The inside of the car was brightly lit, though.

I tried once again to tell her to be patient, but Tohko rummaged through her bag and pulled out a paperback.

I saw the title and gasped.

*Alt-Heidelberg*—!

The book I'd given to Tohko. The one stuffed under her mattress the day I'd nursed her out of illness. When I'd tried to tear it up and make her eat it, she had stopped me with tears in her eyes—

*"Not that book. If I eat it…I won't have it anymore…* Alt-Heidelberg *is all I have left. It's the only one."*

Of the nearly two-thirds of the pages that had been left, she'd gone through more than half.

When I saw that, a sharp pain shot through my chest.

*I said good-bye…I thought…as long as I didn't eat the rest of* Alt-Heidelberg…

When the pages were all gone, maybe Tohko would forget about me. That unresolvable panic welled up in me.

Tohko turned the pages of the book, and in a whisper of a voice she expounded on it.

"*Alt-Heidelberg* is a play written by the German author Wilhelm Meyer-Förster. It was published in 1901. It's a famous story that tells of the joy and sorrow of youth through the meeting of Crown Prince Karl Heinz of the kingdom of Karlsberg—though he's formally called Heinrich—and a girl at his boardinghouse named Kathie. It has a sweet taste, like biting into candied violets...a melancholy taste...a bitter taste...

"As the heir to his uncle the grand duke after his parents died young, Karl Heinz had had a strictly regulated life enforced on him ever since childhood. He winds up studying abroad in Heidelberg, the city of students, and his heart thrills to the life of freedom of a college student.

"Kathie is a girl who works at his boardinghouse. She gives Karl Heinz a bouquet of flowers to welcome him and recites a poem. The two of them quickly fall in love."

Her slender fingers had stopped above the page, not moving. Whenever she talked about a story, she was so excitable and happy, and yet now her downcast eyes were sorrowful and moist.

"His first love...his first days of freedom...He made a lot of friends, too, and experienced days that he would never trade for any price—of such happiness as he had never before known.

"Yes...like the fragrance of violets that spreads through your mouth the moment your teeth break the brittle candy shell.

"But it didn't go on very long...The grand duke's illness worsens and Karl Heinz must cut short his studies and return to his country.

"Two years go by and he's become grand duke. Overcome by nostalgia, he returns to Heidelberg, but it's no longer the Heidelberg he knew."

Tohko's voice was hoarse. At the same time, her fingertips slid hesitantly over the page and stopped at its edge.

She couldn't possibly be in the mood to eat—!

She was being so careless! She would never usually dare such a risk.

99

I heard a *riiip* of paper.

A white scrap between her fingers, she slowly brought it to her lips.

If she ate it, it would be gone! She would forget!

Unable to bear the pain crushing my chest, I stretched out a hand.

I stuck my hand between Tohko's lips and fingers and squeezed her hand to stop it there.

It was impulsive and startled Tohko, too, and she abruptly shut her mouth. She bit down hard on the soft part at the base of my fingers.

"—Rkk!"

"Konoha!"

Tohko pulled back quickly.

She set the book in her lap, clasped my hand, and rubbed the reddening bite marks with her fingers.

"Why did you stick your hand out all of a sudden? Oh no, you can see tooth marks. That must have hurt…"

The thought occurred to me that this was the second time she'd bitten me hard enough to leave tooth marks, and in an angry tone I told her, "Because you were going to eat the book."

Maybe she sensed something in the emotions packed into my voice. Tohko looked up at me with sad eyes. I glowered back at her even more fiercely.

"Why are you eating it?"

"Well, it won't keep forever. If it gets too old, I won't be able to eat it anymore. And you bought it for me."

She spoke to me in a tone like an older sister lecturing her unreasonable little brother, and through irritation that seemed to scrape at my chest, I got indignant and grabbed the book off Tohko's lap.

"E-even so—you're not supposed to eat in trains. I don't care how much of a glutton you are, you should know better. What if someone saw you?"

Tohko drooped dramatically. "...I'm sorry."

My throat burned painfully. I felt desolate and antsy, and I didn't understand myself very well anymore.

What did I want to do? What did I want to say?

I turned my eyes away and glowered sulkily at the bite marks Tohko had left on my hand. Then suddenly, Tohko put a finger to the furrow in my brow.

She peeked into my surprised face and whispered, "That's an awful wrinkle."

"Wh—!"

"Is what Kathie says as she strokes the face of Karl Heinz, who's grown tired of his role as grand duke and come back to Heidelberg."

Her braids swung and the scent of violets tickled my nose.

A warm smile came over Tohko's face and she softly stroked my forehead.

*"Come on, give me a smile again."*

Her gentle fingers slipped from my forehead to my cheek. She touched me gently, as if to cheer me up.

*"Once more the way you did before. Smile, Karl Heinz. Come on, smile for me."*

Tohko's eyes were reflected in mine. Her pure gaze, like a violet—

My cheeks grew hot, as if a fire raged within them, and at the same time my chest filled with melancholy, and then I, too, opened *Alt-Heidelberg* and began to read Karl Heinz's lines.

*"Kathie, everything was how it used to be—the Main, and the Neckar, even Heidelberg. Only the people had changed. There's no one here who's the way they used to be."*

I was sure when I thought back to this later, I would be embarrassed to death and roll around on the floor in my room.

But that was a hundred times better than watching Tohko eat the book I'd gotten her down to the last page right in front of me.

A look of surprise came over Tohko's face; then her eyes immediately grew sad.

"*You're the only one, Kathie. The only one still the way they used to be is you.*"

Tohko smiled in silence.

It was a smile so pretty that it squeezed my throat tight.

My voice caught naturally.

"*—You're the only one—*"

My heart clogged up and I could no longer speak. Tohko gave me a bright, teasing smile, and then she stood up smoothly and shifted to my side. She wrapped both hands around my arm and pulled me toward her, then read Kathie's next line.

"*Go on then—I still remember the day you departed—we had decided to go to a forest in the Odenwald together.*"

I nodded, following the stage directions.

Tohko's eyes gleamed even more teasingly.

"*And then we would ride in a carriage to Neckargemünd—and after that would be Paris. Remember?*"

The stage direction said, "*She smiles,*" and Tohko followed along, crinkling her eyes.

At the next direction, she even pressed her face to my chest.

I felt Tohko's weight directly above my heart, and my head spun at the fragrance of violets wafting from her hair. *You're taking this too far, Tohko! Why do you have your eyes closed so serenely?!*

Unable to follow suit, my breathing weak, I read my lines.

"*Outside there was a spring storm that night. Everyone was asleep.*"

Tohko raised her face and gazed at me, enraptured.

*"You held me tight, I remember."*

When I saw the next direction, I jolted to a stop, brutally shaken up. Argh! This scene was no good!

There, I saw written, *"(He catches her up and kisses her passionately.)"*

Tohko had become Kathie completely. She was leaning against me and looking straight up at me with a syrupy gaze.

My brain was boiling, I descended into breathing problems and an irregular pulse, and I closed the book and set it on the seat.

"I can't do it. I'm sorry."

Tohko pulled away from me and bobbed over to the seat opposite. She picked the book up as she went and giggled.

"You were a wonderful prince, Konoha."

I groaned, my shoulders slumping completely. Tohko was watching me in amusement.

Then she rested her back against the seat and closed her eyes contentedly.

"Thank you. That filled me up."

Her face was serene, as if she'd just had a joyous dream.

She hugged *Alt-Heidelberg* to her chest and kept her eyes closed the rest of the time.

Had she fallen asleep? Or was she pretending to be asleep?

I gazed at the flowerlike smile on her lips with aching, melancholy feelings.

Thinking about what might have happened if I had followed the stage directions and caught her up and kissed her…

We transferred to the bullet train, and by the time we arrived at Tokyo Station, it was nearly eleven o'clock at night.

We left the station and walked for a bit; then Tohko stopped and said, "Thank you for coming today. We can split up here."

"It's late. I'll take you home."

"No, I'll go home by myself. Let me do that."

The words were uttered with a smile, but they were a clear refusal.

A cutting pain ran through my chest.

It confirmed my belief that Tohko really was trying to distance herself from me, and the world went dark.

Even though she'd been so close to me a little while ago! Even though she'd smiled the same way she used to! Even though she'd leaned against my chest and closed her eyes in contentment!

"Good-bye."

She turned her slender shoulders and began to walk off. I shouted out to stop her.

"Tohko! What do you want me to do?!"

My spirit was a mess, my throat burned, and I couldn't breathe well. I didn't know what I should do.

Tohko turned around.

She looked me in the face and, troubled—sadly—she wrinkled her brow.

There was a pungent spasm in the back of my throat, the depths of my heart rocked, and as I approached tears, I begged, "I don't want to write a novel! I don't want to become an author! And I can't write the story like manna that your mother would have written! But—but…if I wrote, would you stay forever? You wouldn't go anywhere?"

The wind rustled her long braids. Tohko's eyes crinkled, her heart seeming to wrench as she listened to what I said.

If Tohko were to tell me right now that she wanted me to write, if that's what she wanted, if that's what would change her future—if I didn't have to lose Tohko—

I—

I would—!

Tohko was the one who stopped the words that threatened to explode from my mouth.

"It's fine."

When her limpid whisper fell on my ears, I couldn't believe it.

Like Alissa telling Jerome she was leaving, Tohko was looking at me with a transparent gaze and smiling kindly.

"I wanted to read my mother's stories again. I wanted to fill my empty stomach with them. I thought that everything would change then and go in a better direction. I thought maybe you'd be able to do it."

A subtle shadow fell over her eyes.

"But that was a selfish desire..."

Her voice wavered sadly. A smile pulled at the corners of her mouth again almost immediately.

"So it's fine. I'm sorry for lying to you up till now."

She clenched her hands into fists against her legs and bowed her head deeply.

I was frozen in place, still on my feet.

All I could do was bug out my eyes and gape.

When Tohko raised her face, she said, "Good-bye," with a gentle expression, and then left.

Her delicate body melted into the darkness.

*"It's fine."*

Those cruel words echoed in my ears long, long after.

⟶⬧⟵

**Alissa talked about it in her diary, remember?**

**That the path God pointed to was narrow and could never be walked with another—**

I'm sorry, Kana. I never actually had the right to wish for your happiness.

Because I was the one blocking your way to happiness after all.

When Tohko was born, I was finally liberated from suffering.

And Fumiharu would embrace me when I embraced Tohko, and say, "I'm sorry," and treat me kindly.

My world turned back to light and hope, and I was content, as if I were dreaming on the near side of a broad gate.

I had Tohko and I had Fumiharu. Peaceful, warm, average, and obvious.

But you won't come over to me!

All you do is stare frigidly when Tohko eats the stories I write, just like Alissa would never go anywhere, even though she knew, *"There are countries like that."*

Can't you hear me calling anymore, Kana?

Won't you read the things I write anymore, Kana?

If you would walk to meet me—I would give you anything I had, if you told me that's what you wanted.

⋙◆⋘

I don't know how long I stood there.

The sense of loss was stronger even than the cold of the wind striking my cheek.

My mind fuzzy, I pulled my cell phone out of my pocket and checked my alerts.

While I was on my way to Iwate, I'd gotten a text from Akutagawa saying that he'd met up with Kotobuki without any problems. I'd sent a text to Kotobuki's phone then, too, to apologize, but I still hadn't gotten an answer. She was probably ticked off. It was understandable.

The only text I'd gotten was from my mom, which I'd answered, telling her that we couldn't come back for lunch after all. She'd seemed worried and asked, Did you have a fight with your girlfriend? and told me, Don't let it get you down!

When I pulled up Akutagawa's number and called him, I heard a girl's voice.

"Konoha?"

The fog that had settled over my mind was blown away instantly.

"Miu?!"

Why was Miu on Akutagawa's phone?! And at this hour? Visiting hours at the hospital should've been over a *long* time ago.

Miu responded to my stupor with a taunting voice.

"I heard you blew off your date and ran after Amano. What an awful thing to do. Your girlfriend was crying like crazy. She was saying she hates you and how she's going to break up with you."

"N-nuh-uh! I didn't say that!"

Suddenly another voice broke in. *Kotobuki?*

"What? But I thought you were swearing up and down that you were done with an unreliable guy like that and that you never wanted to see his face again?"

"No, I didn't! That's a lie! Don't believe her, Inoue."

What was happening? I could hear Miu's voice alternating with Kotobuki's voice. I stared into space, unable to grasp the situation, when I heard Miu's voice saying unhappily, "Hey! Kazushi! Give that back!" Then came Akutagawa's voice.

"...Sorry, but it doesn't look like we'll be able to have a casual talk on the phone," he said, sounding disgusted. "So why don't you come over? Kotobuki and Asakura are both here, too."

When I went through a magnificent, Japanese-style gate and walked up to the front door, Akutagawa met me with a vaguely haggard look on his face.

"Did you manage to find Amano?"

"...Yeah, it was nothing major."

"Oh. That's good."

"Sorry to put you to all this trouble."

"I don't mind that, but..."

Akutagawa frowned. Still standing at the front door, I asked in a low voice, "Why are Miu and Kotobuki here?"

"Actually...I had plans to go out with Asakura today."

"What?! Really...I'm sorry! I didn't know—"

Apparently after he got my call, he'd called up Miu to say he wanted to cancel their plans. As it turned out, Miu threw a fit and he wound up having to explain the situation and Miu had proclaimed that she was going along.

When Akutagawa told her he didn't have time to pick her up—*"Okay, I'll head over and wait with Kotobuki. Girls need to be together at a time like this. You're not going to be able to tell her anything that'll help anyway."*—she'd decided unilaterally and he hadn't been able to refuse.

"And actually, Kotobuki was incredibly depressed, so it was a good thing that Asakura was there."

They'd moved to Akutagawa's house after that, and the two girls had gotten into it with each other, just as they'd done when they answered the phone.

"It got late, so they both decided to stay here tonight. My dad is gone for work and both my sisters understand. We got permission from the hospital and my sister called Kotobuki's family, so there's no problem."

Akutagawa's face was tinged with fatigue.

"Er, I...I'm really sorry for causing all this trouble."

As I began my apology, a voice sounded from the top of the stairs.

"What're you doing, Kazushi? Konoha's here, isn't he? Bring him up here already!"

*Urk.*

"Go on then! Tell him what you wanted to say! Reasonable girls go to the bottom of the priority list. Then they wind up switched out for another girl. Not that I care if that *does* happen to you, of course."

"I-I haven't been switched out!"

"That's true. Even if that's what's going to happen soon, for *now* at least you're his girlfriend. Though it doesn't look like you're getting the girlfriend treatment at all."

The second I set foot in Akutagawa's room, Miu started nudging Kotobuki toward me.

Kotobuki was struggling against her and turned her gaze on me with a troubled, angry-looking face.

"I'm sorry, Kotobuki."

I apologized meekly and Kotobuki's voice choked off.

"You're not seriously going to let him off the hook with just *that*, are you? If you act that indulgent, no question he's going to do it again. You've been getting played for a fool from the start."

"Th-that's not what happened!"

"Wow. Konoha never once broke a promise to me, you know. Not even to go play with his friends. He put me first and turned them down."

"Urk...is—is that true, Inoue?"

"Umm, well..."

"Not to mention weighing another woman against his girlfriend and then deciding to ditch his girlfriend. That's out of the question. If he did that to me, I'd never speak to him again."

"Inoue had his reasons, Asakura. He was really worried about

109

Kotobuki. To the point that he sent me to her. That's proof that he cares about her."

Akutagawa took up the battle for me.

"I really am sorry. Ryuto called me up, sobbing that Tohko was in trouble, so…it threw me off…"

"You get tricked by Sakurai so often, I dunno if you're innocent or if you just don't learn. That's called being stupid."

"…Why don't we excuse ourselves, Asakura?"

"But then there wasn't any point in waiting for him to get here. You can go wherever you want by yourself, can't you, Kazushi? Right, Kotobuki?"

Holding herself up on her crutch, Miu suddenly shoved Kotobuki forward with her other hand.

"Eek!"

"Agh!"

I hurried to catch Kotobuki as she toppled over.

"A-are you okay?"

As I looked down at her, holding her in my arms, Kotobuki's eyes watered and her jaw locked.

A shock went through me, seeing her look as if she might burst into tears any second.

"I…didn't tell you I get superjealous, Inoue?"

"Wh—? Uh…yeah."

Suddenly there was a loud noise and my cheek burned.

Her right hand still in the air, Kotobuki glared at me, lips pursed. I was dazed as she said, all in an angry rush, "You jerk! You're such a jerk! Why did you go see Tohko?! E-even if you do have a reason, it ticks me off…I was looking forward to the movie! And then we were supposed to go to your house afterward—I was looking forward to it…so, so much. And then you did that! I ate all the cookies I brought with me! Even though I made them for you! I hate, hate, hate you! You two-timer!"

She walloped me in the head again, this time with her hand squeezed into a fist.

Behind her, Miu shrugged her shoulders and Akutagawa was gaping.

Kotobuki was panting, her shoulders heaving, when suddenly her face crumpled and her expression became dejected and sad.

"I...I'm really angry. It feels like my chest is going to rip itself apart, I'm so jealous of Tohko."

Hearing those words, seeing her face, it felt like my heart would break apart, too.

I made Kotobuki sad so, so often. Even though she was my girlfriend.

"I'm angry...about a lot of stuff. So I don't mean this forever, but...don't talk to me for a little while!"

She dropped her clenched hand and spun on her heel. Unlike Tohko, her small frame was obviously shaking.

"Y-your bathroom?" she said roughly to Akutagawa. "I need to use your bathroom."

"R-right..."

Akutagawa went with Kotobuki out of the room. She kept her eyes turned away, trying not to look at me. Her face was trembling with frailty, even in profile.

Out of nowhere, I got hit on the cheek again.

There was a sharp *crack*. It was Miu who'd hit me this time.

Her large eyes shone with displeasure. I stood dazed, and this time she scratched me right across the face.

"You're a real professional at hurting girls, Konoha."

"Miu..."

A chill went through my spine at the coldness in her voice.

I felt like there was loathing in Miu's eyes. That fact threw icy water over my body.

"You've still got a spaced-out look on your face. Why don't you wake up for a change? You still haven't picked up on it? Tohko Amano is someone who doesn't exist in the real world."

My heart gave a jolt.

"Is that...from Kanako's novel?"

Her expression still hard, Miu stared straight into my face and said, "Yes, it is. I read *The Immoral Passage*. *Toco is a girl who doesn't exist*—but it's more than that. At the planetarium, she recited the last scene from *Like the Open Sky* from memory. But it wasn't in the book. I wondered how she knew about your first draft, and it bugged me.

"I found out from Sakurai that his mom writes stuff. I never suspected she was Kanako Sakurai. But after what happened at the planetarium, I read your book over again and saw Kanako Sakurai's name in the judge's reviews and that made me realize. Tohko Amano is the baby Toco from Kanako Sakurai's novel.

"And if she had a connection to Kanako Sakurai, then it wasn't strange for her to have read your first draft, either. She would also know that you're Miu Inoue. But she was at your side, hiding that knowledge. *She'd been keeping a secret from you*—"

Akutagawa and Kotobuki still hadn't come back.

Miu's expression grew sharper and sharper. To the point that I thought maybe she still hated me—

"Why didn't she tell the truth? In order to make you write another book, right? The kind president who's been at your side this whole time, protecting you—Tohko Amano who's been with you for two years—is a convenient illusion!"

Her fiery shout rose up alongside the pain that crushed my body.

It wasn't true!

Tohko had kept quiet about the truth, but the kindness and warmth she had shown me were all genuine, too.

And yet I hadn't been able to forgive her one betrayal and had attacked her.

I hadn't tried to understand the pain or suffering Tohko felt, driven to such extremes that control of emotions was impossible. I'd run away, wanting to make myself the only victim. Even though Tohko had always been kind to me—always—and had constantly worried about me!

Miu's face crumpled suddenly and took on a sad, sympathetic look.

"...Don't make that face, like an abandoned puppy. You should face reality sooner rather than later. Because you have a girl who isn't an illusion."

And then her eyes crinkled in an even sadder smile.

"You know...Kotobuki didn't cry once. There were a bunch of times she looked like was about to while she was waiting for you, but she stayed strong in front of us and she didn't do it."

I realized now the reason why Kotobuki still hadn't come back. She was obviously crying, alone in the bathroom, hiding her sobs...

I hung my head and Miu kept talking.

"Konoha, did you know that there's a sequel to *The Immoral Passage*? It's a short story that ran in a magazine and it was never made into a book, but..."

The pitch of her voice grew slightly lower.

"The doll of Toco grows up little by little, even though she's a doll, until one day she moves of her own volition and kills Arisa."

The sliding door rattled, which made me shiver.

I realized that Akutagawa and Kotobuki had returned, and the sweat that had broken out over my skin dried with a shuddering chill.

Kotobuki's eyes were red. When I saw that, a stab went through me.

"Why don't you stay the night, too, Inoue? It's late. Asakura and Kotobuki, you two should head to bed soon. There are blankets in the guest room. You don't mind staying with me, right, Inoue?"

"Thanks. But I'm going to go home."

Her back turned, Kotobuki's shoulders jerked.

Akutagawa knit his brows.

"You won't be able to catch a cab in this neighborhood."

"I'll work something out."

"Use my bike. You can just ride it to school, then."

"Thanks. I'll do that."

Outside, it was bone-chillingly cold. It was nearing one o'clock at night.

"Thanks for everything today, really."

"Be careful. Don't get into any accidents."

I nodded and had set my feet on the pedals when Kotobuki came through the gate, her lips pursed.

"I'll see you."

Akutagawa patted my shoulder and walked away.

Kotobuki's face tightened and she was glaring at me, but she stuck out a hand without a word.

Gloves?

"...Your hands are going to get numb on a bike."

"You brought these out for me?"

Without replying, she whipped her face sharply away.

I accepted them and slipped them on with a feeling that warmed my heart. The cutesy pink gloves enveloped my hands in warmth.

"Thanks."

Her face still turned away, Kotobuki bent her lips.

Then all of a sudden, she said in a blunt voice, "I-I'm still mad, so don't try and talk to me at school or anything. And I'm going in by myself in the morning, so don't wait for me. B-but... if you think you still want to go out with me, then prove it."

"... Prove it?"

Kotobuki looked up at me, glowering, and there was something vulnerable there—and yet she seemed to have planted her feet.

"In return for what I did on Valentine's Day...I want you to call me Nanase on the fourteenth. If you do that, I'll trust you. Until then, I'm not going to talk to you."

She finished her blunt speech, turned her back, and ran off through the gate.

After watching her go with a dismal feeling, I started pedaling the bike.

The dark road, sunk in the silence of night, was like the limitless pitch black of outer space.

As I lightly pedaled, I thought back over what Miu had said with a pain that twinged relentlessly.

*"You should face reality sooner rather than later. Because you have a girl who isn't an illusion."*

*"The Tohko Amano who's been with you for two years—is a convenient illusion!"*

My heart pounded heavily. The breath clinging to my face was lukewarm and white, and though my body was cold, the back of my throat was hot and prickly.

I knew perfectly well who I should choose between Kotobuki and Tohko.

*"It's fine."*

The view of Tohko's resolute frame when she had smiled and turned her back on me and Kotobuki's precariously trembling back came to mind simultaneously and my throat hurt even worse.

Tohko trying to leave me.

Kotobuki coming toward me clumsily, persistently.

Even though there could hardly be anyone *but* Kotobuki who would walk with me down the wide, warm path I wanted.

Why did I end up thinking only of Tohko like this?

*"The doll of Toco grows up little by little, even though she's a doll, until one day she moves of her own volition and kills Arisa."*

What was it Miu had been saying?

A doll killing someone? Toco killing Arisa?

*Tohko killing Kanako?*

No—*that* couldn't be anything but fiction. To think of Tohko, who clung to Kanako almost despairingly, killing her—

I stopped the bike in front of my house.

Someone was crouching down beside the gate, hugging one knee to their chest.

The lamp on the bicycle shone on Ryuto.

He slowly lifted his head, and the face that looked up at me gave me a shock like a slap in the face.

Ryuto was crying.

It wasn't the violent crying like when he'd come to my house before, clinging to me and bawling. It was quieter than that.

Transparent tears fell over his cheeks from wide-open eyes. They were vulnerable tears that seemed to vanish in the air. His

116

hair and clothes were disheveled, and sorrow and tortured pain hovered in his moist eyes along with deep despair.

Was this another trap?

Although this looked nothing like an act. Ryuto seemed so shredded and full of suffering that he honestly couldn't stand. He made no sound; he didn't even twitch. His tears simply continued flowing.

I approached Ryuto, rolling the bike alongside me.

In the still darkness, the rattling of the tires could be heard.

"...What's the matter?"

Ryuto was looking up at me, his tears still flowing. A gaze ripe with suffering, as if begging for salvation, that seemed to say, "If I can't have that, then kill me and let me be at peace."

He whispered powerlessly, his voice hoarse. "Konoha, there's some things...you're better off not knowin'. And once you find out...you can't go back."

A tear dripped onto his knee.

His torn jeans sucked the tear in and changed color.

"I...can't tell Tohko...nngh..."

His throat trembling, he buried his face against his knee and wept quietly.

The sight of him was so agonizing it dug at my heart.

What had Ryuto found out that he was this tortured by it?

"What can't you tell her?"

His face still lowered, Ryuto shook his head from side to side.

I parked the bike in front of the gate and then laid a hand on Ryuto's shoulder.

"Let's go in the house. You'll catch cold."

Ryuto shook his head again and sobbed low.

"Konoha...thank you for chasin' Tohko down today. I can't do anythin' to save her now. I want her to be happy...'cos...'cos she's special. But I can't do it...I've been with her since I was a kid... but when it came down to it, I couldn't do anythin'."

Ryuto's tears were dropping into my heart, too.

With each one, a soft region deep inside my chest burned. The almost irritating sense of melancholy made it difficult to breathe.

Ryuto lifted his face, wet with tears, and looked at me. With a voice that threatened to break off, with an expression that did the same, he pieced his words together.

"Konoha...please write. For Tohko. You're the only one who can save her... Tohko *made her decision* a long time ago. I can't stop her. But you're her author...so if you write...nngh...that's all I'd ever ask."

Sadness washed over my body.

*Ryuto... Tohko told me I didn't have to write anymore.*

She said it was fine.

She smiled quietly and turned her back.

Seeing my face tight and silent, Ryuto seemed even more deeply despondent.

He dropped his head and scrubbed at it, curling into a ball and weeping at my feet.

Finally he stood sluggishly and stumbled off.

"Ryuto..."

Even when I called to him, he never turned around as he departed.

—————◆—————

**Do you think I'll ever be able to see the narrow gate, too, Kana?**

**Do you think I'll have the courage to return everything I own to where it belongs, to say everything that needs to be said, to trust myself to the person I must trust and pass alone through that gate?**

I was brushing Tohko's hair, thinking about that, when suddenly I felt as if my heart was breaking, and I held Tohko in my arms and cried.

Tohko was so surprised.

I told her, "*I love you, Tohko, I love you so much,*" and Tohko did her best to tell me, "I love you, too," and then my chest hurt even more.

"Why are you crying, Mommy? Did you have a fight with Daddy? Did Daddy do something wrong? Huh? Mommy?"

"No…no, it's not that. Mommy's happy. She's so very happy that it made her cry."

I don't know what I should do, Kana.

I'm the one who triggered it. If I hadn't acted so stupidly, nothing would have happened between us.

Fate turned around somewhere beyond my reach.

I know it's not good for me to be with you.

I'll stop you from growing. I'll get in the way.

I know that, but I can't help wanting to be with you.

Like before, just the two of us, forever and ever—

I don't have to write. As long as we can be together, I never have to write a novel! I want to scream that.

God, please never make me say that.

If *that day* comes, I hope that I'll be able to smile sunnily, as if I had nothing at all to be sad about, and go through the gate.

## Chapter 5—The Anguish of Paradise

I put the gloves into Kotobuki's desk along with a note that said, "Thanks."

Kotobuki usually came early, but this morning she came in just before the bell, then kept her eyes turned unnaturally away from me and sat down at her desk. She started to put her textbooks away and must have found the gloves. She seemed to gasp, then pulled the pink gloves out of her desk, and her face fell and became forlorn. Then she hugged the gloves gently to her chest and lowered her eyes.

I watched her, feeling desolate.

The fact that Ryuto had acted so strangely nagged constantly at my mind, too, and I made a promise with Takeda to meet in the library basement at lunch.

Takeda got there first and had spread her lunch over the desk. The container with cartoon characters drawn all over it was neatly packed with bacon-wrapped asparagus and broccoli.

"How can you even eat?"

It was cold and dark and creepy more than anything else... I didn't think it was the right environment for a meal. Takeda dipped her fork calmly and chomped on her chicken fried rice as she said, "I've been drinking tea and eating candy alone for a long time. If you don't eat now, you won't have time to."

"...That's okay. I'll eat later."

Takeda blithely said, "Oh, okay," and split her tea with me. She poured some into the cap of her thermos and then held it out to me invitingly. It was so cold I thought I was going to freeze, so I accepted it gratefully. Today she had jasmine tea.

I saw a paperback copy of *No Longer Human* on the desk and felt a chill, but I started to tell her about Saturday.

Takeda continued eating dispassionately and listened with a face as empty as a doll's. Occasionally she would steal a glance at *No Longer Human*, then go back to eating again.

My story ended right as her lunch box emptied.

"I knew that Ryu called you to make you chase after Tohko. After you left Ryu's house, he called me on my cell phone. Asking if I'd come over to his house."

"When was that?"

"A little bit before noon. He told me to make lunch, so I took some food over. Ryu seemed like he was in a good mood then. He was so happy telling me about how you'd blown off your date with Nanase and gone off after Tohko. He said you liked Tohko better after all."

I knew Ryuto was making me dance, but I didn't like it...I'd hurt Kotobuki again because of that.

Takeda said that after Ryuto had cleared the lunch she'd made, he'd gotten out a photo album.

"Was that the album that belonged to Tohko's mother?"

The album shut away in a closet rose in my mind, and my skin tingled.

"No. It was Ryu's. There were hardly any photos of Ryu's mom. It was all Tohko's family. He told me Tohko's house was like his home. He wasn't particularly sad then, either. He was pretty upbeat."

The anomaly happened in the middle of looking through the album.

Ryuto had been talking and in a good mood up until then, but suddenly he went pale and stared at the album and fell silent.

"His face looked like he'd gotten this crazy shock and he didn't move a muscle. He was just staring at the album. I called his name, but it was like he didn't hear me."

"What picture was Ryuto looking at?"

"Just...a regular photo."

Confusion showed in Takeda's eyes.

"At least, that's how it looked to me. It looked like it was taken in the dining room at Tohko's house on Christmas. Tohko and Ryu and Tohko's dad were sitting at the table. Tohko and her dad were carrying the plate with the turkey on it together and were turned toward the camera and smiling, and Ryu had his arms around a plate with a cake on it, and he looked thrilled. All three of them had on sweaters and Christmas-themed buttons that looked handmade. Tohko's mom wasn't in the picture, so I'm pretty sure she's the one who took it."

A peaceful family get-together on Christmas...I wondered what it was in the picture that had startled Ryuto so badly. Takeda said he'd had his eyes fixed on the photo without even twitching a muscle, and then had groaned out of nowhere.

"He said, *'It can't beee!'*"

Then he'd opened the closet and pulled out a box, almost crazed.

He opened the cardboard box, dumped its contents on the floor, and then hunted through them, crawling on his knees. He repeated that act several times and then suddenly stopped moving again.

"And then Ryu said something."

"What?"

"He said, 'It wasn't Yui?'...and his face was pale, like he might die any second."

I gasped.

**It wasn't Yui?**

Did he mean—the one who'd used the poison? But then who *had* used it?!

Or had there never been any poison at all? Had the Amanos died in an ordinary accident?

"Ryu left with this incredibly tortured look on his face and I had no clue what was going on, so I was just staring at the front door. Then Ryu's mom came home."

"Kanako!"

"Yeah. She had a *seriously* scary look on her face, and even though I said hi, she went into the house without saying a word to me. It looked like she was annoyed about something and in kind of a rush."

Why had Kanako gone home? Tohko had said, "...*She wasn't at home today, was she?*" which meant she hadn't planned to be home on Saturday. And yet...

Given Ryuto's behavior, I had no clue what was happening, just like Takeda.

Takeda said she'd gone back to her own house after that.

"I called Ryu's phone a bunch of times, but he never picked up and he never answered my texts. So...he went to your house, huh?"

"He asked me to do something for Tohko."

Takeda laid a hand lightly on the cover of *No Longer Human*.

"That sounds like a last request."

The words, whispered with her cold face, made me start.

"What are you saying? Of all people, Ryuto would never commit suicide or anything like that."

"I don't know. Ryuto is broken down. He bawls his eyes out to girls over nothing...then when you push him away, he whines and gets mad and cries. How can he live with just his emotions, doing whatever he wants? I can't understand it. I kind of...hate him a little."

An emotion sharp like a splinter of glass came into her empty face, then disappeared.

That flash gave me goose bumps.

Takeda's hand didn't move from atop her book.

In the end, it still wasn't clear what had happened to Ryuto.

When I visited Maki at her workroom in the music hall after school—"Oh really? Hmmph. Was he that messed up, the little boy?"—she opined haughtily as she faced the canvas and moved her paintbrush.

"Well, he's always doing whatever his whim tells him and acting flippantly. It's obnoxious. So it's good for him to knock his head against a wall and spray some blood around every now and again. Otherwise he'd just turn into an even more intolerable punk."

She was being free with her opinions, even though he was supposedly the father of the child inside her. When I asked whether Ryuto had been there, she replied, "If he had, I would have chased him off," and so I was at a loss.

"I wonder why men are such wastes of humanity. They're almost always as fragile as they are swaggering. They crumble in a second. I'm going to be angry if he goes into hiding or dies on me. What a pain."

Her eyes bugged with anger, and she seemed pretty annoyed.

"Umm, Ryuto's not dying, though."

Takeda was one thing, but why did Maki have to take the conversation in unnecessary directions? Though on Saturday night,

Ryuto had certainly been as feeble as a sick, cast-off puppy when he huddled outside the gate of my house.

"No, I'm talking about another idiot."

"Another…?"

In a dark voice, Maki muttered, "Tamotsu Kurosaki."

I gasped.

"He's pretty much stopped eating since Hotaru died. He looks like a skeleton. Because of which he's destroying his company. There aren't enough words for how pathetic he's become."

I recalled the stormy, tragic love when I saw her rage-filled gaze. Heathcliff without Catherine…

He had been the guardian of the young girl named Hotaru Amemiya, had been her uncle by marriage and her lover, as well as her father. The last time I'd seen him was the day of her funeral.

Skeletal, a stubbly beard on his face, his sunken eyes flickering with agony and despair that could never heal… That day, he had been the very image of Heathcliff wandering the moors in search of a fragment of his soul.

He had committed an unforgivable crime.

He had looked as if even he didn't hope for salvation any longer. Like a ghost, simply waiting endlessly through hunger and thirst for the end of the world to come.

"That man…has abandoned his business, secluded himself in his mansion, and has been starving himself to death. Despite the fact that he killed someone to seize the company and did plenty of dirty stuff to make it grow. It looks like it's going to be taken over by another company. And still he doesn't have the energy to fight! If he dies like that, Hotaru would turn in her grave."

I gulped at her scathing tone. Her eyes, glaring fixedly at the canvas, burned like fire.

"I'm serious." Maki groaned, gripping the paintbrush so hard that she shook, and then she shouted spitefully, "You think I'm gonna sit by and let him die?! I slapped him until my hands swelled up, over and over, punishing him. I will *never* forgive him if he dies! Thinking about Hotaru! Tasting suffering more bitter than death! Even if the weight of his many crimes presses on him and stops him from breathing, he has to go on living!"

Unforgiving of the weakness in Ryuto or Kurosaki, Maki was like a perfectly straight, unbending sword.

Even if she despaired, Maki would probably never give up living and fighting.

I was so jealous of that strength that my chest burned.

I left the music hall, and as I walked through the school yard, I thought things over bleakly.

If I had someone like Maki who would give me a firm order when I was stuck at a crossroads, maybe I would be able to go in that direction unhesitatingly.

If I was ordered to live when I was on the brink of death, maybe I would be able to stand back up.

But Tohko always made me decide in the end.

Each time I hunkered down, she would gently squeeze my hand. But she would never pull me by the hand and lead me to the right path.

She would simply get a warm smile on her face and look at me and ask, *"How do you want to do this, Konoha?"*

*"What do you think, Konoha?"*

*"What do you want to do?"*

*"Where do you want to go?"*

\*　　\*　　\*

126

The white sheets and smell of medicine in the nurse's office—as I covered my face and cried in bed, Tohko whispered sadly.

*"You have to find the answers to those questions on your own, Konoha. Even if it hurts…even if it makes you sad…even if you suffer along the way…you have to get there on your own."*

But I couldn't find the path on my own. I didn't know which way I should go.

I went into the school building and changed my shoes at the shoe locker. My foot slipped and I fell.

How could I fall here where there was nothing? I couldn't even support my own body. No strength would go into my legs…

A tear dropped.

I had only stumbled a tiny bit, and yet sadness welled up to fill my throat, and feeling embarrassed, my breathing pained, restless, I stood up shakily and started walking, like a child searching for its guardian.

My feet carried me to the book club room automatically.

Even though I knew Tohko wouldn't be there. Even though it would only hurt to go there.

I didn't know anywhere else to go. Tears dropped onto my palms.

*"Hello, Konoha."*

When I opened the door, Tohko, sitting on a chair by the window with her knees pulled up to her chest, turning her face toward me and smiling, rose up like a vision and I felt dizzy.

The fold-up chair was empty, and the scenery outside the window was misty and white.

The old books piled up on the floor had lost their reader and transformed into useless paper.

I buried my face against the pitted wooden desk where I had always written Tohko's snacks, and I cried.

Tohko wasn't here.

I'd known that and yet sorrow stabbed at my chest and my throat quivered.

The days I'd spent with Tohko pressed in on my chest, one after another.

Smiling beneath a magnolia tree and puffing out her chest, saying, *"As you can see, I am a book girl."* Tugging on my hand while I stood gaping, bringing me to the book club room to make me write improv stories as snacks. Tearing the pages into tiny pieces and bringing them joyously to her lips. I had listened, sliding my mechanical pencil across the paper, to the secretive *crinkle-flp* sound, to her voice when she gulped it down and began to expound.

Why had Tohko always, always seemed to be having so much fun when we were together? Why had she smiled so happily?

When she suddenly announced that she was taking a break from the club to study for her college exams, that day, too, she had eaten a snack from the mailbox in the school yard—*"That was delicious!"*—and left a letter about her reactions.

She was utterly, completely hopeless at math and had gotten Fs on it, and yet when I was having problems, she would come and help me without fail.

The smell of the wooden desk pricked my nose as I pressed my face against it. No matter how much I cried, the tears kept coming.

Tohko's face rose in my mind.

Ryuto had said that there are some things it's better not to know. I didn't know what it was he'd learned.

But I'd never wanted to find this out, either. What a pathetic, useless person I became without Tohko.

I'd hoped I would become someone who could look straight

at the truth, and yet I'd been bowled over by my own weakness being laid bare and broke down crying.

That day at the planetarium, I'd been determined to finally move into the future.

Under a tree at a factory on the outskirts of town on Christmas Eve, Tohko had squeezed my hand, and I'd returned to the time in my life when I had wept pathetically. That night I'd felt the warmth of Tohko's hand and thought about the phantom who had departed all alone, and I'd prayed that he and Kotobuki and Miu would be happy—

I learned then that the truth wasn't always beautiful.

The music teacher who'd taught me that nothing beat an ordinary life had been a sad criminal, who, more than anything, had lusted for talent, had envied talent, had been driven mad by talent, and he had even laid hands on his lover.

The truth hurts people.

Salvation doesn't exist anywhere.

Even a young man with the voice of an angel, spilling over with radiant talent, could become a phantom spattered in filth and sunk in the shadows of night.

I wondered what had become of him...

*"Do you think Miu Inoue will write another book?"*

That young man who'd questioned me with a sorrowful look in his eyes—

*"Take care of Nanase."*

He'd whispered that in my ear and then disappeared into the darkness—

I wonder if he passed through the narrow gate, wearing a dauntless expression that seemed to shake everything off.

I wonder if he'd gone alone.

Omi was like me—but he had run down a road I couldn't take without ever turning around.

If Omi were here now, I knew he would wallop me. He would probably never forgive me for hurting Kotobuki.

Even though he liked Kotobuki, he'd chosen a solitary path without telling her anything. I couldn't be like him.

Being by myself, I was lonely.

By myself, I was weak.

When I was sad, there would be no one to comfort me. No hand to squeeze mine. I would have to stand completely on my own.

If I didn't have someone with me—no, if I didn't have Tohko there for me, I couldn't stand back up.

I couldn't walk down any path at all!

I lifted my face, sloppy with tears, and pulled over the fifty-page notebook that had been tossed on the desk. While I sniffled and my shoulders shook and I panted through my burning throat, I gripped my mechanical pencil and turned back the cover.

If I wrote a novel, maybe Tohko would come back.

If I wrote a sweet story the way Tohko liked—not a weird story to tease her like I usually did—if I could write a story that would make Tohko happy, if I wrote a story like Tohko's mother—

The thick lead stopped above the white lines.

What was wrong? My hand wouldn't move...

The first line wasn't filling in, try as I might.

I tried desperately to force the words out, to the point I thought my head would split, but not a single letter came.

I was floored by that fact.

Why?! I'd been able to write so easily before! Nothing was coming! It was as if my body was empty. That shouldn't be. I should be able to write. I'd never been unable to write before, not once. Even when I'd loathed writing and fled from it, I'd always been able to do it when I wanted to. I'd written snacks for Tohko every day!

And yet I couldn't write! My spine shuddered with cold. No—if I didn't write, Tohko wouldn't come back. I had to write—a story like manna falling from heaven!

The lead in my pencil snapped apart. I clicked it in a panic, but no matter how often I pushed out new lead, it kept breaking before I could write a single letter.

A bleak feeling came over me and I started to have trouble breathing. The pencil fell from my numb fingers.

There was a tight pulse in my temples, and taking shallow breaths, I slid out of the chair onto my knees on the floor.

I had thought I wasn't going to ever have an attack again.

Tears fell again at how pathetic and mortified I felt. Sweat broke out in torrents, and the intervals between breaths grew smaller and smaller. Air wasn't getting into my lungs at all!

I was suffocating. It hurt. I should just die here! I don't want to be where Tohko isn't!

Just then someone squeezed my hand.

They said something near my ear.

*Tohko—!*

It couldn't be her, and yet the voice sounded like hers. Tohko was holding my hand, stroking my back, and encouraging me.

*"It's okay. It's okay, Konoha. I'm here. Everything's okay now. Try to breathe a little slower. That's it, slowly... and let it out. That's it. Good... it's okay."*

*"It's okay. It's okay."* The words I'd once heard Tohko say, whispered again and again in my ear.

My breathing gradually stabilized and my sweat dried.

Through my hazy vision, I could see a small hand squeezing mine.

*... Tohko?*

131

No, it was someone else.

Tohko's fingers were more slender. And they were pale.

Whose hand was this?

When I sluggishly lifted my face, eyes as cold as a doll's were looking at me.

"...Takeda?"

"That's right," she answered in a composed voice.

"...Have you been the one holding my hand this whole time?"

"Did you think it was Tohko?"

When I couldn't answer, she murmured in a voice holding no emotion, "...You called her name. *Tohko, Tohko.*"

So that's what it was. It hadn't been Tohko after all.

And that voice had been an illusion, too.

Takeda let go of my hand and stood up.

"But since you realized I'm not Tohko, it looks like your attack has subsided, so that's good. Do you want to go to the nurse's office just in case?"

"No, I'm fine now. Thanks."

"You don't look very fine."

Again I couldn't answer. I stood up, trying to turn my face away. I felt uncomfortable being seen like that.

"...Why did you come to the clubroom, Takeda?"

"I thought you might be here, so I stuck my head in. That's when I saw you twitching on the floor."

"...Oh."

"We were talking about Ryu at lunch so I couldn't ask, but did you and Nanase break up?"

"...We might end up doing that."

Kotobuki had told me that she wanted me to call her Nanase on the fourteenth. That if I did that, she'd trust my feelings for her.

But the way things were right now, there was no way I could say her name.

132

"Are you not happy with Nanase?"

"I'm not happy with myself. It isn't her..."

My chest ached sharply.

"I'm always confused...I can't even decide which direction to go on my own. I don't have any qualities that would...make Kotobuki like me," I murmured in a husky voice, my eyes still turned away. I hated myself so much I wanted to throw up. My sweat dried and I felt a chill. "I wanted to be a little bit better as a person."

Takeda was silent.

"Maybe people can't change after all."

"You're stabbing me in the back when you say that," a cold voice said beside me.

That voice that held no emotion sounded as if it had been packed with emotions that couldn't be held back, and I turned away.

Takeda was looking at me with her empty eyes.

"You're the one who told me that even I might be able to change if I went on living, even the way I am, and you gave me hope."

I was cut through the heart and left speechless, looking at Takeda's face.

She was right.

A searing regret welled up in me.

I'd told Takeda that I wanted her to live.

I'd told her that she had to reach a different place than Shuji Kataoka, whose life as a mime behind a mask had come to an end when he took his own life—

Takeda slapped me crisply on the cheek.

These last few days, I'd been slapped by three girls—Kotobuki, Miu, and Takeda.

I stared blankly at her. Takeda looked at me with eyes cloaked in a faint heat, then said, "This time I'll be the one who teaches you. People change. I want you to come with me now. There's someone I want you to meet."

## Chapter 6—When the World Ends

Where in the world were we going?

Takeda didn't say a word on the bus. Who was it that she wanted me to meet?

We got off at a stop I didn't recognize and I followed hesitantly alongside Takeda as she went down a broad walking path.

The sky was dyed with a gentle sunset.

I could feel that the air, which had seemed freezing cold a short while ago, had grown ever so slightly warmer. The weather reports had said that spring was right around the corner.

The area around us had the feel of a growing neighborhood with rows of apartment buildings. All of the buildings were new.

I heard a baby laughing, so I looked in that direction and saw a young mother sitting on a bench in a park lush with trees, apparently on her way home from shopping. She was peeking into a baby carriage at her side, playing with her baby.

The mother's gaze was placid and kind.

Wait—

I'd seen that woman before.

I didn't think there were any women I knew who could have

had a baby. Her name wouldn't come to me, either. But I was sure I knew her from somewhere...

Her short-cut hair swayed gently around her slender neck.

The baby reached a hand out of the carriage and she squeezed its fingers gently, a slight smile curving her lips, and she started talking to it.

I looked to my side and saw Takeda had her empty gaze fixed on the mother and baby.

Then the memory of a roof on a clear day in May surfaced in my mind.

*"I knew you were the one who killed Shuji.* **You** *were S, weren't you?"*

A voice ringing out with denunciation under a piercing blue sky.

Takeda had exposed herself to the murderer who'd revealed his true identity, and she had glared at him and yelled fiercely.

But it had been someone else who Shuji Kataoka called "S."

She had once been the manager of the archery club and was now someone's wife and was about to give birth—

Rihoko Sena—

No, Rihoko *Soeda*!

Of course, that was Rihoko!

She'd cut her hair and looked very different, so I hadn't been able to tell. Was the baby in that carriage the one who'd been inside her that day? So Rihoko had given birth to the baby!

But where was her husband? Where was Soeda?

My pulse had risen out of shock and panic.

Takeda had been convinced that Rihoko's husband, Soeda, had been "S," and she'd sent him threatening letters. Soeda had had

135

an intense inferiority complex about Shuji Kataoka during high school, and he'd stabbed him with a knife on the roof.

But Shuji hadn't died. Rihoko's words that *"No, you're no longer human"* became a trigger pulled, and he'd thrown himself off the roof.

Rihoko had never told her husband about that.

When she became his wife, she had known that he'd stabbed Shuji and that he'd gotten afraid and tossed the knife away and that he'd fled from the roof, and she'd known about the bleak, helpless emotions Soeda felt for Shuji.

When he heard Rihoko's confession, Soeda had wept, *"It would have been better if I **had** killed him."*

He had wept, why had she married him when she'd loved Shuji? How was he supposed to live with her now, when they were going to have a child? It would be hell!

Takeda had watched the two of them with cold eyes, like a soulless doll.

"Rihoko."

All of a sudden, a placid voice called out in our ears.

The sinking sun cast a fresh scarlet over the benches, the swings, the jungle gym.

A long shadow stretched over the ground.

Leather shoes approached leisurely. A gray suit, a light jacket.

Eyes crinkled in a kind smile behind pair of glasses was Soeda.

A sweet smile came into Rihoko's eyes, too, as she met his gaze.

Soeda bent at the waist and lifted the baby out of the carriage. He brought his face close to it and told it, "I'm home." The baby laughed loudly.

Rihoko pushed the carriage and Soeda carried the baby, walking toward us talking in low voices.

Rihoko was the first to notice.

She saw us and murmured, "Oh," and then Soeda turned his eyes toward us, too, and a look of surprise came over his face.

Takeda smiled innocently, like a puppy.

"Hello. We were in the area, so I thought I'd come with Konoha. You told me before that you come to this park a lot with Nozomi to wait for her dad."

Rihoko and Soeda's faces both softened.

"Only when he comes home early."

"If I came home at this hour every day, I wouldn't be able to feed my family."

They both had placid eyes, as if they were completely different people from the day I'd met them on the roof. The baby was making noises and squirming in Soeda's arms.

"Inoue…"

Soeda looked at me, and his face became apologetic.

"I did something truly inexcusable to you. Something was wrong with me that day. You looked like Shuji and…I'm sorry."

My heart skipped a beat, and I shook my head quickly.

"Forget it ever happened. So you named your baby Nozomi, huh? It's a girl?"

Soeda's eyes calmed. He looked down at the baby as if he was gazing at something he couldn't help but treasure.

"Yes. She brought us together."

His tone was visceral, as if savoring the thought. Soeda told us about everything that had happened.

How it had hurt him to even see Rihoko's face for a while, and he hadn't returned home for several days in a row.

Even after her due date approached and Rihoko went back to her parents' home in Niigata, he never once went to see her.

Rihoko talked, too.

How she'd been extremely uneasy before Nozomi was born.

How she'd been at the point of giving up, sure that she would never be able to repair her relationship with her husband.

Even after Nozomi was born he didn't come to the hospital. She was nearly crushed, sure that it was truly over between them, and she'd been unable to sleep at night.

The day she was released, Soeda was standing outside the hospital.

"Honestly, I'd gone there to talk about getting a divorce. But when I saw Rihoko holding Nozomi against her chest—when Nozomi turned to me and her face lit up—my feet carried me to them naturally and I hugged them both together. It was then that I could finally believe we would all share our lives."

Tears were forming in Rihoko's eyes, as well.

"I knew it, too—that we were going to be able to be a family."

Something warm welled up from deep in my chest.

It made my heart rock wildly.

That day at the beginning of summer—as Soeda wept on his knees on the roof, Rihoko had gone on murmuring to him, her face calm, as if all emotion had dropped from her.

*"We will live the rest of our lives in hell. It's not so bad; as long as you're prepared for it, you can live anywhere."*

*"We'll go on with our peaceful, everyday lives, forever thinking about Kataoka, forever his prisoners. We'll have this child and raise it. We'll live in hell from now on. That will be our atonement to him."*

Rihoko had told him, *"We will live...in hell."*

When she'd uttered those words that day, Rihoko had been terrifying.

But she'd been suffering for a long time, too.

The crime wouldn't go away. They couldn't pretend that the wrong they'd perpetrated had never happened. She'd said that they had to live normally and at peace even so, embracing that suffering and pain.

Only now did I understand, to the point of trembling, that those words had revealed Rihoko's resolve.

And then also, why Takeda had brought me here.

*"People change.*
*"... This time I'll be the one who teaches you."*

The couple who had been plunged into the utter darkness of despair, distrust, and atonement were spending their days peacefully, carrying the burden of their sinful past.

Even knocked flat, gouged out, and defeated—as long as you're alive, change will come. If you grit your teeth, set your resolve, and take one step forward—

Takeda, who had wept for me to let her die, also peeked into Nozomi's face and smiled brightly.

It may have been a false smile, desperately constructed; even so, she was smiling—normally, happily.

My heart churned at that smile. That someday she would be able to make the lie true—

We were invited to dinner and politely declined; then we retraced the road we had come by.

As we waited for the bus at the stop, illuminated by the light of a streetlamp, Takeda said with a cold face, "You won't stay knocked down forever, either, Konoha."

Then she added starkly, "Ryu, either..."

She thought about it a little, then shook her head.

"No...maybe Ryu *will* be down forever. But...when I destroyed my heart, he was nice to me...I'll be able to do that without a second thought, with nothing to gain...When he's sad or lonely, I'll be nice and spoil him. I'll smile from the heart, happy..."

Takeda's voice grew softer and softer until finally she fell silent.

Maybe Takeda's feelings for Ryuto were slowly changing, too.

That's what I thought, but I didn't say it. Takeda would probably realize it for herself someday.

Though maybe she already had...

I had to change, too.


After school the next day, I went with Akutagawa to visit Miu at the hospital.

Miu was going to be released next month.

"I'm shocked to get a visit from you, Konoha. Did you come to ask me to mediate between you and Kotobuki?"

She sat beside the bed and looked up at me teasingly. When I offered her the gift I'd brought of black tea pudding from the store she liked, her face shone with a little excitement.

"You've come to see me before, right? So this time I thought I'd come see you."

At that she smiled even more excitedly and accepted the pudding.

"Hmmph. I see."

"Thanks. For coming to see me again. I wanted to tell you that. And that you've changed. Uh, I mean that in a good way obviously."

"Is that all?"

"Huh?"

"For something like that, you have to say, 'You're so much more charming than before.' Flatter me."

"Oh, uh...sorry."

"Don't apologize when I tell you that! Geez, you're as blind as ever to how girls feel. That's why you're burning through Koto-buki's patience."

"You're pushing it, Asakura."

"You're such a nag, Kazushi. Be quiet and eat some pudding or something."

Miu roughly shoved one of the puddings I'd brought at Akutagawa's chest.

Then she peeled back the lid of a pudding, too, and still fuming, she scooped some up with a plastic spoon and started to eat.

"Why am I surrounded by worthless guys?"

After that complaint, she suddenly turned her eyes away and her tone of voice became awkward.

"But... I wanted to apologize, too. For going too far before. So I'm glad you came today."

Miu's cheeks were red.

After fidgeting hesitantly for a bit, she held some pudding out to me, too, told me to eat it, and then continued speaking curtly.

"You know, Konoha, the novel you wrote really did hurt me. If you hadn't written that novel and applied for the new author prize, I might never have experienced that level of despair. I might still have been at your side, deceiving you... hating and loving your stupidity and innocence. But you know, Konoha."

Still holding her pudding, Miu looked up at me.

Her eyes were straightforward and filled with the sincere desire to tell me this here and now.

"Your novel also saved me.

"When I heard the real final scene that you'd written for me in that planetarium, it felt as if the hatred and sadness in my heart were melting away. I thought, *Aaah, I've wanted Konoha to say this to me for so long.*

"The words you gave me were very, very beautiful. I'm sure that

I'll think of them when I'm having a hard time in the future. And then I'll be able to keep fighting."

Light shone into my heart like sunlight through trees.

The words Miu spoke had also tolled a bell of warm celebration over me.

My lips curved into a smile.

Someone's words could make me this happy and give me strength.

"Thank you. This is the first time I can be glad I wrote that novel. Thanks to you, Miu."

Miu turned her face away in embarrassment again.

"Hurry up and eat your pudding. Geez. And what are you doing just holding your pudding and spacing out, Kazushi?"

"...Asakura." With a serious face, Akutagawa informed her, "I can't eat it without a spoon."

"—Urk. You've got to speak up about stuff like that sooner!"

"Sorry. You were telling a nice story, so I didn't have a chance to interrupt."

"Argh! You should have just taken one and not said anything, then."

Miu threw the entire bag with the spoons in it at Akutagawa. He took a spoon out and handed it to me.

Apparently Miu had secured permission from her parents to live on her own. Akutagawa was apparently going with her to look for apartments. It turned out that Akutagawa's requirements were even more exacting than Miu's, and she was the one who was actually going to live in the apartment. He complained that it had to have automatic locks, that she needed surveillance cameras, that that place was close to a slot parlor and didn't seem safe, and she wasn't making any decisions, so it was getting to be a lot of trouble and he was getting upset.

"And where exactly would suit your tastes?"

"I would have the least to worry about if you would rent a room at my house. We have a spare room."

"What are you talking about?! Are you serious?" Miu wailed, red-faced.

I laughed. "Akutagawa's gonna be an overprotective father. There's going to be trouble if you guys ever have daughters."

"Hey now, Konoha! Why do you have to start talking about kids over something like that? You're acting like Kazushi and I are together."

She glared at me ferociously and I flinched.

"N-no, it's just that yesterday I saw the baby of someone I know. It was a girl and she was really cute. Her name's Nozomi. You write it with the characters for 'hope' and 'beauty.' Her dad picked it out as soon as he saw her."

Rihoko had told us with an effusive smile that it was the name Soeda had given her when he'd embraced Rihoko and their baby in front of the hospital after chasing after them from Tokyo.

It was at that point—

Something tugged at my mind.

Wasn't there something similar between Rihoko's story and the story of Tohko's mom that we'd heard at the hospital in Iwate?

The nurse had talked about how Fumiharu also hadn't made it in time for the birth because of work...

That Yui had seemed anxious about giving birth alone, that she'd looked worried about something...

They'd decided that if they had a girl, they would name her Tohko—that her mother had seemed truly happy—no, that wasn't it. The problem was something else.

There was another—

That's it: *the fact that Yui had a child at a hospital in Iwate.*

*The fact that Fumiharu was in Tokyo for work and couldn't go visit her.*

But Fumiharu's coworker Mr. Sasaki had told us that before Tohko was born, Fumiharu would rush home when evening came to look after Yui. That he had sidelined his work and he was restless while he was at the office, and everyone had teased him.

Yui was in a hospital in Iwate.

Fumiharu didn't go visit her.


*So then who was Fumiharu going to see after work?!*


The insides of my mouth grew suddenly dry.

In *The Immoral Passage*, the author Arisa and the editor Haru weren't in a romantic relationship.

Kanako had told everyone that she and Fumiharu had a "chaste union."

But could Fumiharu and Kanako have had romantic relations? Could Fumiharu have been having an affair with Kanako during Yui's pregnancy? Or maybe even earlier!

And wasn't Yui sad when she was in the hospital?

An image came to mind and goose bumps rose all over my body.

It couldn't be—! That was what Ryuto had meant! *The one who used the poison—!*


"Is something wrong, Konoha?"


Miu's face scrunched up as she asked. I heard her voice at a distance.

"Sorry! I forgot that my mom asked me to run an errand. I should get going."

144

I made a faltering excuse and left the hospital.

As I walked, head bent, down the tree-lined path while sunset closed in, my heart raced as if threatening to tear itself apart.

Tohko had told me that the morning the Amanos died, Yui and Ryuto had eaten normal food and Fumiharu and Tohko had eaten a "meal" that Yui wrote for them.

That Fumiharu and Yui had drunk coffee that Fumiharu had brewed.

How had I overlooked something this important?

If that was the only thing they'd both consumed, that would mean the poison had been added to the coffee. The one who'd brewed the coffee was Fumiharu.

*Which meant, the one who'd poisoned them was—!*

The core of my brain was on fire.

Ryuto's words echoed disturbingly in my ears.

*"Konoha, there's some things...you're better off not knowin'. And once you find out...you can't go back."*

Why had Ryuto been in such despair? *Was it because he'd found out it wasn't Yui or Kanako who'd poisoned the Amanos, but Fumiharu?*

The ambiguous, dreamlike scene Ryuto had talked about drunkenly.

*"She stuck a spoon into the coffeepot and swirled it around... and the silver dust spun in a smooth circle, dissolvin' into it."*

*"... When I tried to help her put it in the cups, she told me I was too little and I might hurt myself. Then she picked up the coffeepot and poured it into some cups with flowers on them. That's when the earth cracked open and turned dark."*

145

Hadn't Ryuto been watching Fumiharu brew the coffee, at his side?

It may well have been Yui who'd hidden the poison in the heart-shaped violet bottle in her jewelry box. And maybe, like Ryuto had said, the one who'd given it to her was Takumi Suwa, who'd died in a car accident.

But the one who'd brought the coffee to her was Fumiharu. Could Ryuto have convinced himself in the confusion of memory that the one who'd brewed the coffee and the one who'd poured the coffee were both Yui?

And yet he'd realized.

That Fumiharu was the one who'd ended it all—

*"...Someone points at a shelf—and they tell me. The sleepin' powder of Ole Lukøje is up there—"*

As Ryuto pointed into the distance with a shaking finger, Fumiharu's face, which I'd only ever seen in photographs, overlapped with his. A gentle smile—

I didn't know what it was in the Christmas photo that had given Ryuto such a shock. Or what he'd been searching for after.

But if Fumiharu had had an affair with Kanako and Yui had suffered because of it—what if Fumiharu had known that Yui had poison? What if Fumiharu had been beset with guilt and used it?

*What if the one who'd planned the murder-suicide was Fumiharu and not Yui—?*

Just like in the novel Kanako wrote, fantasy and reality mixed together chaotically in my mind. A variety of emotions intertwined, eddied together murkily, and I could almost but not quite glimpse the truth.

None of it was more than conjecture.

As I walked quickly, panting, I pulled up Ryuto's number on my cell phone and called him.

I got his voice mail again.

"This is Inoue. There's something I want to talk to you about in person. Could you give me a call?"

And then I headed for a place Ryuto frequented.

I wonder what would happen to Fumiharu if he took poison. Would he die? Or, since he's *different* from us, would he be fine?

When we were all eating together at home, I asked that because my heart had reached its absolute limit.

*"I have the sleeping powder of Ole Lukøje. I would hate it if I was the only one who went to sleep and Fumiharu was the only one who stayed awake if we took the medicine together."*

I said it as a joke, but I prayed for it to be that way.

I wanted to sleep eternally and let Fumiharu be free.

That day, you glared at me with a pinched-up face, Kana, and Fumiharu answered with a laugh.

"I guess I won't know until I have some. Though I think as a living creature we should have a certain amount in common as far as poisons and medicines go. But for myself, I would hate for my end to come dying from poison someone fed me. If I'm going to die anyway, I want to die for something more important."

"Like what?"

"I live with the writings of authors as my nourishment. So I want to give something back.

"I want to become the nourishment for an author's writings. That's why I chose to be an editor.

**"If I were to die, I would want that death, too, to be the nourishment of someone's writing. When I die, would you write about it for me, Kanako?"**

**Fumiharu's eyes were gentle and dreamy.**

**You told him irritably, "Don't talk about such stupid things!"**

**Even so . . . you probably will write about it.**

**You would write about our deaths, if we were to die.**

———◆———

After I got to the restaurant, I left my second message on Ryuto's voice mail. Telling him that I was at Harumi's restaurant and I wanted him to come.

When Harumi brought over the milk tea I'd ordered, she was worried about Ryuto, too.

"Ryuto's been acting funny lately. He's always had this quality like a big, unruly kid, but his mood swings have been especially bad lately. I wonder what happened to him."

I called my mom to tell her I didn't need dinner and stayed at the restaurant until nearly nine.

During the day it was a fast-food restaurant, but at night it turned into a bar and the number of customers coming to drink increased steadily, so I was forced to leave.

As I walked alongside the roadway illuminated by neon lights, I was trying to call Ryuto again when—

I caught sight of Ryuto himself right in front of me.

A shiver went down my spine.

He looked even more wasted, like his mental balance had crumbled even further than when I'd seen him on Saturday night. He looked tormented by suffering, as if he'd abandoned everything, just like Kurosaki had at Amemiya's funeral. He looked like a ghost, wandering aimlessly. His steps were light and unsteady, and he didn't seem to know where he was, or even where it was he was trying to go.

"Ryuto!"

When I ran up to him, he looked down at me with languid eyes.

Had he not showered this entire time? He stank of sweat.

"...Konoha."

"Great, so you got my messages?"

"...Messages?"

"You didn't?"

"...I threw my phone away."

A lump stuck in my throat.

Ryuto's voice was incredibly hoarse, his panting breaths were uneven, and his bloodshot eyes never focused on anything. Deep in his black eyes, maddening pain and despair flickered like a fluorescent light being shut off.

"No one...is willing to kill me. They all say they love me or they adore me or whatever, but when I ask them to kill me, they get all scared and run away."

He took several shallow breaths as he murmured indifferently, but I shuddered.

"My kid...is gonna be born in the fall, y'know. If I die now, I wonder if I could get reborn inside that kid. Get born from Maki's body. Call my own mom 'Maki.' Do the whole thing over again."

Cold sweat ran down my spine. There was no end to the electric charge, as if blades were running along the back of my neck.

Ryuto's eyes...*shot*...to the road, and he whispered, "I see a cat."

A car with its headlights on was screaming toward us. I didn't see anything that looked like a cat, and I didn't hear one, either.

"What are you talking about, Ryuto?"

Ryuto had his eyes fixed on the road.

"See it? Over there. There's a black cat in the middle of the road mewing..."

Takumi Suwa was hit by a car trying to protect a cat—Maki's words came back to me and my heart went cold.

I didn't think he saw a cat, but did he think that he could?!

Like a sleepwalker, Ryuto started to take unsteady steps toward the road.

"Wait! There isn't any cat, Ryuto!!"

My shout was erased by the sound of an engine. Ryuto wasn't stopping. He just kept going.

I reached out a hand and was trying to grab his shirt when—

"Ryu."

A cheerful voice called his name.

Takeda was standing in front of Ryuto wearing a milk-colored coat. Her hands were clasped behind her back, and she was looking up at him with an adorable, puppylike expression.

Everything after that was like a slow-motion scene on TV.

The corners of her mouth still curved into a smile, Takeda drew closer.

With a glint, a knife appeared from behind her back.

And with it

She stabbed him.

Deeply—into Ryuto's chest!

The knife she held was the folding knife that Kotobuki had tossed aside in the underground storage room.

He'd been trying to leap into the road, and she stabbed him, as if to bind him to this place, to drive a wedge into him to hold him back!

He couldn't believe it. That's how it looked when he opened his eyes wide and looked down at her.

Takeda gripped the knife she'd plunged into his chest firmly in both hands and smiled brightly, her eyes syrupy.

It was a kind, sweet smile.

Ryuto's eyes crinkled as well.

The corners of his mouth pulled into a wisp of a smile, and his expression grew peaceful and fulfilled, as if this was the happiest moment he'd ever lived.

The sounds around us grew distant.

Any number of cars drove past the two of them.

Ryuto reached out an arm and pulled Takeda close. He put his cheek against her fluffy hair, breathed in the scent of it, and for one moment his eyes looked pained, on the verge of tears. Then he smiled again slightly and closed his eyes, as if he was being called into the most blissful rest.

Ryuto collapsing against Takeda...

Takeda crouching in the road with Ryuto circled in her arms...

Her face transforming into emptiness like a doll's...

The blood seeping from Ryuto's chest spreading steadily over the sidewalk and passersby screaming—

I watched the entire tragedy, all of the love happening right in front of me, in mute shock.

—————◆—————

**I don't want to make anyone write anymore.**

**But there are people whose destiny it is to write.**

**People who must continue to write, taking hatred, suffering, sadness, death and the loss of people important to them—even topics like that as their nourishment.**

People who try to reach the pinnacle known as God by doing so.

Is it a curse? Is it a blessing?

Kana.

What can I do for you?

If I was to disappear completely from this world, would you love Tohko and Ryu?

Would you be happy with Fumiharu for me?

I lose in the gamble.

I'm sorry that you suffered for such a long time.

Good-bye.

## Chapter 7—To the Person I Love Most

Ryuto was taken to the hospital in extremely serious condition and went into emergency surgery.

Takeda was sitting on a chair in the lobby, her expression vacant. I tried to talk to her, but she never responded. In the ambulance she'd murmured, "I wanted...to give Ryu the thing he wanted most."

Maki rushed to the hospital and yelled, "How stupid could he be?!" her face twisted. She bit down hard on her lip and irritation and panic showed in her eyes, but she was issuing orders over every last detail to Takamizawa, and she told me to go find Tohko.

"Leave this part to me and bring Tohko here! I am *not* going to let this kid follow Ryuto into suicide, so go *now*."

Even when Maki said that right in front of her, Takeda didn't offer the slightest reaction, which gave me a stabbing sense of unease. But I headed for the Sakurai house in a car that belonged to Maki's family.

When I'd called from the hospital, nobody had picked up, but there were lights on in the window.

I went as far as the front door; then when I was reaching for the doorbell, the door abruptly slid open and Tohko came out look-ing harried, carrying a pale violet-colored box in her arms.

"Aunt Kanako!" she shouted, and then her face tensed and she became flustered. "I-I'm sorry. I heard a car stop so I thought it was Aunt Kanako... What's going on, Konoha?"

"Takeda stabbed Ryuto and he's seriously hurt!"

When I told her that, her eyes grew wide and the box fell from her hands.

It made a thud and sky-blue and rosy scraps of paper scattered out the door, were caught in the wind, and blew around.

Were these the letters I'd seen before?! Why were they torn into such tiny pieces?

Tohko's knees buckled. Her face was pale. She picked up one scrap of paper and whispered feebly, "...I have to get Aunt Kanako."

The next instant, she stood up with a look of determination.

"Hold on," she said hurriedly, withdrew inside, and then immediately returned.

While we were heading to Kanako's office in the car, Tohko kept her head bent, brooding.

"She might not see me. She might never forgive me. She read the letters..."

She wasn't talking to me. It was as if she was confounded inside herself and suffering. She would look down at the scrap of the letter she clutched in her hand again and again, then bite her lip.

I tried to cheer her up by telling her we'd left a message on Kanako's answering machine, so she might be on her way to the hospital by now, but Tohko shook her head.

"No, she won't go," she whispered in a hard voice, staring fixedly at her knees. "There's only ever been one person who's important to Aunt Kanako. Since that person's gone, she's not going to love anyone ever again."

Was that person Fumiharu?

"But this time—*this* time I have to bring her. Otherwise she and Ryuto will be beyond help forever."

As soon as the car stopped in front of the apartment, Tohko opened the door and rushed out.

We climbed the stairs, and when she reached the outside of Kanako's apartment, she plastered herself against the door and rang the bell.

"Aunt Kanako, open up! It's Tohko! I know you're in there!"

There was no response.

Tohko's face twisted in pain; then she pulled a key out of her pocket and put it in the door.

A copy? It must have taken guts to use that. Kanako would definitely get upset. Even I could picture it. Even so, Tohko set her jaw, turned the key, and opened the door.

She took off her shoes and went deeper inside. I followed after her.

I could hear the *clack-clack* of typing on a keyboard from ahead. Something squeezed tight somewhere around the pit of my stomach, and it became difficult to breathe.

Kanako was facing a computer with a chilly expression. Even when Tohko called to her, her slender fingers continued moving, and she didn't so much as turn her eyes.

"I'm sorry I let myself in. Ryuto's in the hospital. They said he was stabbed in the chest and he's unconscious. Please—come with us to the hospital!"

Tohko shouted desperately. Her staring eyes and her loud voice were both spilling over with gut-wrenching pain.

But Kanako faced the screen, her gaze never shifting. Unable to stand it, I yelled, too.

"Please, Kanako! Ryuto is really in trouble!"

Kanako opened her mouth for the first time. Without shifting her eyes, she informed me coldly, "I have a manuscript I have to finish by tomorrow. You're bothering me. Go home, *Inoue*."

She was determined not to hear anything Tohko said. Her staunch, absolute refusal sent a chill down my spine.

Even at a time like this, this woman—

Tohko stared at Kanako, her face twisted with pain, and she begged, "Aunt Kanako...Ryuto is dying."

"It won't save him if I go, will it, *Inoue*? People die when it's their time, and there's nothing I can do about it."

What a horrible person! What an absolutely awful person!

I didn't know if the thing welling up in me was anger or fear or despair.

"Aunt Kanako, you're Ryuto's mother..."

"...Ryuto doesn't think of me as a mother," Kanako murmured as if to herself, to no one in particular.

"You're wrong! Ryuto has always wanted you to smile at him and hug him!"

"...When he was little, that boy was glued to Yui far more than he ever was to me. Even when I was home, he never came near me."

"That's...that's because you kept him at a distance! Because you told him he couldn't even call you mom! So he never got attention from you. But he wanted to call you mom. When he was little, he would tell me, 'It's so cool how you can call Aunt Yui mom.'"

The cold clatter of typing filled the room.

Even though the person she was talking to was right in front of her, Tohko's words rolled off Kanako's back like she existed in another dimension. She couldn't even acknowledge her presence.

Desperately holding herself up on legs that threatened to fail, Tohko was no longer the book girl who fixed her wise eyes on the truth and gently read out its story; she was just a powerless girl.

Sadness surged up in me at how hoarse her voice was. It sounded like it might break.

"Ryuto loved his mother more than anyone! He wanted her to love him!"

Her voice shot straight into my heart.

The person Ryuto loved most.

The person at a distance whom he had adored since childhood, whom he could never have.

In that instant, I knew who it was!

Knew who Maki's arrogant gaze; who Takeda and Amemiya's vacant, unseeing faces mirrored; *who it was they had resembled—!*

A stream of words and images streaked through my mind.

The photos in the album that had fallen out of the closet, the two girls standing in front of an art museum in the woods, the violet barrette, the cold eyes, Ryuto pointing and saying, *"Ole Lukøje's sleeping powder is up there, the silver dust pouring out like sand."* What Mr. Sasaki had said, what Ryuto had said, what Tohko had said, what we'd heard the nurse at the hospital say—

The blood boiled in my body and rose to my head all at once. In the midst of violent dizziness and confusion, the scattered pieces all came together, as if blown into place by a sudden wind.

I advanced to stand beside Tohko.

"What Tohko's saying is true. Ryuto loved you more than anyone. He told me that. He said that Tohko's mother was his first love."

"He meant Yui obviously," Kanako muttered in exasperation.

"No, it was you. You're Tohko's real mother!"

Kanako looked at me in surprise. Tohko gasped, too.

Even I was flabbergasted and confused, and I was the one who'd said it.

How could Yui and Tohko not really be mother and child?

So then had Tohko received such cruel treatment from her real mother? Had this woman ignored her real daughter? Had Ryuto continued to love her even so? While burning with twisted hatred, obsession, and love?

The air became harsh and taut. Fired by a hot wind whirling inside my body, I pressed her.

"We visited the hospital in Iwate where Tohko was born. The nurse who saw her said she looked just like her mother.

"But Tohko and Yui's features *aren't that much alike*. Even Mr. Sasaki told me that the way they laughed and the impressions they gave off were identical, but he never said a word about them resembling each other physically. The one who resembles Tohko more than Yui is you, Kanako!"

Their hairstyles and the vibes they gave off were totally different, so I'd never noticed.

But seeing them both up close like this and comparing them—their eyes, their noses, their lips, the whiteness of their skin, and their slender builds were so like the other's that it would be unnatural for them not to be related.

I'd seen in photos that in middle school, Kanako's black hair had been straight and cut short above her shoulders. If she grew her hair out and put it in braids, she would look even more like Tohko.

Kanako was glaring at me with glacial eyes. They made me think I could hear the moan of a blizzard in my ears.

"I heard Fumiharu would go home early to take care of Yui before Tohko was born. But the nurse said Yui gave birth alone! So then where was Fumiharu going after work?

"*He was spending his time at home with Yui after all.* You

were the one in the hospital!" I declared unequivocally. "You gave birth to Tohko *as Yui*. There'd been a romantic relationship between you and Fumiharu. Tohko is your and Fumiharu's daughter! Ryuto realized it, too, seeing your and Tohko's faces in the same house all the time. He realized that you were Tohko's mother and Tohko was his sister by blood—"

That was all the more reason that Tohko was "special" to Ryuto.

Tohko must have known, too. That's why she'd gone to the hospital to confirm it. No matter how she was treated, she couldn't hate Kanako.

Tohko listened to me speak with a frail look on her face.

How must it have felt to be continually treated as a "nonexistent child" by her real mother? How had she dealt with that despair? Just imagining it made my chest constrict.

Kanako spoke in a sharp voice.

"You think I took on the part of Yui to give birth? Why would I need to do something so convoluted as that?"

Her gaze as she stared at me was like needles of ice. They lanced into me. My mind was taken up by the transformation in Kanako's expression.

"...The fact that Yui was pregnant is established from Mr. Sasaki's statements. So then where did *Yui's baby* disappear to? In *The Immoral Passage*, your counterpart Arisa strangles the baby Toco. After Haru and Yuiko's deaths, Arisa finds only a doll and Toco's corpse at their apartment—

"But you can't actually hide a baby's body. So then *maybe the baby was never born?* Maybe Yui had a miscarriage."

Kanako's face was taut. I fixed my gaze even more directly on her.

"The child who should have been named Tohko no longer existed. That's why you gave your child the name Tohko and gave her to Yui. In order to save Yui—"

Kanako gritted her teeth and I saw her eyes flash with loathing, and I felt sure that what I was imagining was right.

The reason Fumiharu had hurried home was not to care for his wife who was close to giving birth, but instead because he couldn't leave his wife's side after her miscarriage. Yui had probably been in no condition to be left unsupervised.

And perhaps Kanako had also been the cause of Yui's miscarriage—

"Ridiculous. I hated Yui!" Kanako shouted, spitting the words out.

Tohko's face crumpled as if she'd been hurt by that, and she clutched her skirt tightly in both hands.

My spirit wavered for a moment, too.

The wall that stood in front of Kanako was high and forbidding, and it wasn't going to be broken down easily. I could see the answer, but I couldn't communicate it to her. Everything was rejected. Even the words I unleashed were repelled by a cold blade.

But seeing Tohko with her head bowed, looking on the verge of tears, I thought, *I've got to do this.* Tohko had experienced this pain for a long time. I had to break her chains of sorrow here and now. I would drag the truth out of Kanako.

I cut into Kanako straight on.

"That's a lie. You're a liar, Kanako!"

Tohko's shoulders quivered, and she looked up at me.

Kanako's gaze burned with rage. If I was the way I used to be, I would have quailed at such harsh eyes and faltered. But the fear I'd felt toward her up until now had blown away in that instant.

My brain burned. The inside of my chest was thrumming.

"Since it looks like you can't talk to Tohko, I'll make you talk to me instead."

My words were nothing more than the playacting of a child. Even so, I had to get it across.

To this author of ice. Right now, me, with my words!

"I read your book. It was a story I never could have written.

"They say you and the Amanos were the models for it. But you mixed in some author's liberties and completely altered the truth. In the story, Arisa feels that Yuiko's husband, Haru, has a kindred consciousness, and she becomes obsessed. Saying they share the goal of the supreme novel. Because of that, she thinks Yuiko and Toco are obstacles and she hates them. Yuiko is jealous of Arisa, too. But the reality was different."

Kanako's expression changed from fire to ice. Her eyes were bitingly cold and their pupils were vacant.

"No, it wasn't. She would be beaming on the surface anytime at all, but underneath that she was ugly and jealous. And yet she pretended to be a good girl and clung to me and it was miserable."

I asked her, "Really?"

Though I donned a calm air, my heart was uneasy and my gut hurt, as if it was twisting into knots.

How could I knock the walls down? Could I expose the truth within?

Could I change the dark, sad story into a story of love and kindness the way the clear-eyed book girl had shown me up till now?

Tohko stared at me with an intense gaze, as if she was praying for something.

Tohko had told the stories for me on a sunny day at the beginning of summer, in a church in the middle of the night, at a shadowy estate, on a stage with crowds of people watching, on the floor of a moonlit factory, below a starry sky twinkling with stars.

Her long braids swaying, gazing at whomever she faced without fear, a smile on her face—

The sight of her came up vividly on the insides of my eyelids.

I sucked in a breath and calmed my heart.

All right. It was going to start here.

"In *Immoral Passage* you have Arisa say that Yuiko is Juliette married to Jerome. Haru is Jerome and she's Alissa.

"Gide's *Strait Is the Gate* is the story of Jerome dedicating his heart to Alissa and of Alissa, who rejects his love and passes through the gate that leads to God. Juliette has love for Jerome, but her feelings aren't reciprocated. In Jerome's story, Juliette is nothing more than a supporting character. Jerome's gaze is turned exclusively on Alissa. But what were things like from Alissa's perspective?"

It was what Tohko always said.

There isn't one way to read a story. As many characters as there are, there are that many different stories.

*"That's why I try to read stories over again with the feelings of different characters. Because when I do that, it gives birth to new stories."*

*"When I notice something I never noticed before, it feels like discovering treasure."*

In the soft, golden light, Tohko, sitting on a fold-up chair with her feet pulled up, turning the pages of a book propped on her knees, telling a story in a clear voice.

No, the story I was about to tell wasn't Jerome's story.

It was the story of Alissa and Juliette.

"—Alissa and Juliette were sisters, but they were total opposites. Quiet, devout Alissa and cheerful, flippant Juliette. If Alissa was holiness, Juliette was worldliness—but actually, Juliette was also a wise girl deeply intimate with poetry and music. Juliette withdrew from Jerome for Alissa's sake and became the wife of a man who asked for her hand. Meanwhile, Alissa knew how

Juliette felt and she, too, refused Jerome's proposal. The two of them were sisters who were dear friends and considerate of each other that way."

Tohko had told me that Kanako and Yui had been best friends since middle school.

There had been photos of the two of them in that album that had fallen out of the closet, too.

They were constantly together. Yui smiling, Kanako with a cold gaze—

Kanako had said that Yui was an annoyance.

That she'd hated Yui.

But then why had she stayed with her?

Why, even after they went on to separate high schools and then out into the world, had she continued to be at her side? Shouldn't Kanako have been able to cut her ties with Yui, since she didn't fear being alone? So then why didn't she?

"The sisters' relationship starts to change with Juliette's wedding. At first it was a loveless marriage. But over the years, she becomes attached to her husband, adapted to her husband, and stops playing piano and reading. Alissa disapproves of that and writes a letter to Jerome. She suggests that Juliette is only putting on a play of being happy and asks whether in doing so she might have started to honestly feel that way—"

*"As it happens, the thing making my little sister happy is something very different from what she once thought about and different again from what we thought her happiness would attach to."*

*"…Ah, why does the thing we call 'happiness' have such a deep link to the soul? And how valueless are the many things which seem from without to give it shape?"*

*     *     *

"When Juliette was nearly ready to give birth and Alissa went to visit her, Alissa was overtaken by an inscrutable gloom and she couldn't be at ease. Could it be that Alissa was saddened at how her little sister had been changed by marriage? Feeling as if the sister who'd been in the same world as her had gone off to another realm?

"In Jerome's perspective, not much is written about the details of Alissa and Juliette's day-to-day lives. But we can imagine that for the shy Alissa, Juliette, the sister who shared her blood and was always nearby, was someone that she could allow into her heart. Reading books and sharing their impressions of them, Alissa listening to Juliette playing the piano, exchanging gifts on Christmas or birthdays, occasionally talking about the future— they might have spent their time like close friends."

Kanako was looking at her computer screen with a gaze as silent and frozen as the midwinter sky. Not even her eyelashes or fingertips made the slightest movement.

I wove my words together.

"They say the inspiration for Alissa was Gide's wife, Madeleine. She was his cousin, two years older than him, and she resembles Alissa in a lot of respects, but she was a woman who was not exactly Alissa. Are you familiar with the diary Gide wrote about his married life with her, Kanako?"

Her face still turned away in a profile as beautiful and sculpted as a statue, I posed this question to her.

Gide's hidden diary, which I'd read at the library.

What was written in it was the thorny conflict of Gide's soul over the fact that he loved Madeleine but couldn't be one with her physically.

"Gide was gay and he couldn't love his wife physically, so their marriage was a 'chaste union.' While Gide was on a trip with someone he was having an affair with, Madeleine burned all his letters and they had a misunderstanding. Even so, even after her death, Gide continued his pursuit to understand Madeleine.

"Women who resemble her appear repeatedly in his writings. Madeleine is the wellspring of Gide's creativity. She was an irreplaceable presence."

Kanako maintained her silence, her lips pressed together, and so I crisply declared, "You and Yui were Alissa and Juliette! And at the same time, you were Gide and Madeleine!"

Kanako still didn't move. Her heart was shut tight, sealing her words in. That was how she waited for her opponents to wear themselves out, to lose heart and go away.

Did she think I was going to give up?

"Kanako, you felt as if Juliette pulled away from you when she got married, and it made you feel lonely, didn't it?

"I heard that you would constantly summon Fumiharu to your office on days off. They said your relationship with him was a 'chaste union.' I'm sure there was a powerful bond between you, the author, and Fumiharu, the editor. Fumiharu was also the one who discovered you and sent your maiden novel out into the world.

"But the one you truly loved wasn't Fumiharu; it was Yui, wasn't it? And you called Fumiharu to your office in order to make *him* jealous, not Yui, and to pull the two of them apart."

Why had she stayed at her side even after their schools and positions had changed?

Had she been that obsessed?

The suffocating atmosphere drew out for a long time. Kanako still wasn't breaking.

My hands were sweaty.

"When I came here the other day, you had a lot of photos on

your desk. There was also a flower-patterned teacup, a strawberry tart, purple spoon rests...

"Somehow, it didn't fit your image and it stuck with me."

I stole a glance at the simple black mug on her desk.

"You're not using that cup today?"

Kanako, who'd kept her mouth pressed shut, finally said something.

"...People can change what cups they use depending on their moods. They can also get a sudden craving for something sweet."

"The photos on your desk that day were all of scenery—where were they taken?"

"...They're just background material that editing put together for me."

"But I felt like I'd seen that scenery somewhere before. Especially that art museum surrounded by woods."

I said it slowly.

"That's somewhere you and Yui visited on your middle school trip, right?"

Kanako didn't answer.

"The other pictures of schools and streets probably have some link to Yui, too. I saw the same buildings and scenery in Yui's photo album, so that's why I had a feeling I'd seen them before."

Surprised, Tohko asked, "How do you know about my mom's photo album, Konoha?"

Starting to feel awkward, I apologized. "I'm sorry. When I took a blanket out of the closet, the album fell out. I didn't mean to look at it, but... I just happened to see it."

"...I didn't know that," Tohko murmured, her eyes swimming around as if there was still something on her mind.

Just then, Kanako's voice overlaid itself on ours coldly.

"All schools look alike. Besides, what's so strange about having photos of famous tourist spots as background material?"

My face tensed.

"That's true. If it was just the fact that you had those photos, there wouldn't be anything strange about it. But there's something else I noticed."

Kanako glared at me penetratingly as I stepped closer to her. I stopped right in front of her desk and tapped my finger lightly on it, right next to the black mug.

It made a hollow sound.

"You had a spoon here before, right?"

A slight crimson was coursing through her cheeks, which had been as pale as ice. I didn't turn my gaze from it.

"You had a silver teaspoon and a purple spoon rest shaped like a heart."

Kanako pressed her lips together firmly and looked away.

"In the picture at the art museum, you were wearing a blue glass pendant. And Yui had a barrette shaped like a violet in her hair. Its petals had the same shape as your spoon rest. Did that used to be Yui's barrette?"

"Mom's...barrette!" Tohko shrieked quietly. Then she began talking in a daze. "I knew it! Mom had a barrette shaped like a violet. Aunt Kanako gave it to her, and it was really important to her!"

Fierce irritation and panic came into Kanako's eyes. Though my chest burned at the reaction I'd finally managed to drag out, I pursued her even further.

"Maybe I'm mistaken. Could you show me that spoon rest again? We can have Tohko confirm whether or not it's her mom's barrette, too."

"Why is there any reason for me to do that?!"

Kanako's voice was wild at last, and she fixed a glare on me. I raised my voice, too.

"If you can't show us, that's the same as admitting it's Yui's barrette! You went out of your way to make it into a memento of Yui and kept it all this time! You took it out on the anniversary of Yui's death and with photos of your memories with Yui—maybe even the cup and cake Yui used to like—you grieved Yui's death! You were wearing black that day! You meant it to be for mourning!"

Kanako banged both hands down on the desk.

"Get out of here! You're wasting my time forcing me to listen to your ridiculous theories!"

"Theories! No, this is only what I *imagine*. But it's affecting you. You can't answer why you kept such precious hold on a keepsake of Yui when you're supposed to hate her! Making something that touched another person's hair into a spoon rest isn't normal! You'd have to have some especially strong feelings for that person!"

"Get out!"

"No! You loved Yui more than as a best friend. The one you were in a chaste union with was Yui, not Fumiharu! The way Gide loved Madeleine! Yui was someone you absolutely couldn't do without in your life! And Yui was—"

"Yui hated me!!"

Kanako stood up with a clatter and shouted, as if beating us with her naked emotions. The eyes glaring at me were less like ice and more a fiercely burning fire. Flames scattering bright red sparks and spreading out endlessly!

Hidden beneath a mask of ice, her true nature, its intensity—its insanity—was overwhelming.

"That's right! Yui was jealous of me! She was always watching me, nervous that I might take Amano from her! In the end, she took poison and killed herself!!"

How much pain, screaming, hatred, love, and despair had this woman kept locked in her heart?

Ryuto had spoken painfully of how his first love was someone who couldn't be happy.

*"She got betrayed in a way that could never be taken back, by someone she trusted. She fell into a black, lonely darkness...and it ate away at her heart."*

The greatest betrayal for Kanako was that Yui chose death.
Even now, Kanako thought Yui was the one who had used the poison.
But it was—
I started to open my mouth, but then Tohko shouted beside me.

"You're wrong! You're wrong, Aunt Kanako! My mom didn't use the sleeping powder of Ole Lukøje!"

Tohko was shaking. She shouted, her hands balled up, her eyes narrowed in pain, her face pale, as if she was speaking words that tortured her.
"—My mom would never use it...*She didn't use it!* She wasn't the one who added the poison. She wasn't capable of that. And anyway, the one who made the coffee was—that morning, the one who added the poison was—"

"The one who put the poison in the coffee was Ryuto."

Tohko looked up at me as if she'd been shot. Kanako was gaping, too.
No wonder. These last nine years, the two of them had each thought someone different added the poison, and they'd suffered because of it.
"...Everything was an unfortunate misunderstanding."

The act on that morning nine years ago—feeling a pain in my chest that almost seared the flesh, I began to tell the story.

"The morning the accident happened, apparently Tohko and Fumiharu ate a story that Yui wrote for them. You're aware that Fumiharu ate books and that his daughter, Tohko, inherited that trait from him. That day, Fumiharu didn't eat any *normal food*, but he shared some coffee with Yui. Fumiharu had brewed it."

Kanako took a breath. She had probably realized that no one but Fumiharu could have added the poison in that situation.

I'd thought so, too, at first. I'm sure Tohko had as well—

"...You said Ryuto added the poison, Inoue," Kanako murmured in a puzzled voice.

"Yes, I did. Ryuto was the one who mixed the poison into the coffee Fumiharu brewed."

"Why, Konoha? Why do you think that?"

"...Because I've heard Ryuto talk about his memories from his previous life."

Even more intense confusion came over both of their faces.

I told them how Ryuto had said he was the reincarnation of Takumi Suwa.

Why had Ryuto convinced himself of that?

Because he had "memories of his past life."

Memories of getting hit by a car to protect a cat, being taken to the hospital, and dying alone.

Memories of giving Yui, who'd always been kind to him, the purple vial that held the sleeping powder of Ole Lukøje. Memories of Yui pouring it into the coffee.

Ryuto "remembered" things that he should have had no way of knowing, as if his soul could traverse time and place freely.

"But were those things that Ryuto had truly experienced as Takumi Suwa?

"Maybe it was only that his memories of the accident were

things he heard from the people around him when he was little and they stuck in his mind and felt like memories from his past life.

"You could also imagine that the reason he called Tohko's mother 'Yui' was because Yui told him, 'Your dad used to call me Yui.'"

"So then what about his memories of the violet heart-shaped bottle?

"Is it possible that Ryuto might have actually seen it? And then with a child's curiosity, he might have picked it up—"

Tohko suddenly put both hands to her mouth, and in a quavering voice, she whispered, "I-I told him about it! How I saw my mom resting a violet heart-shaped bottle in her palm late at night and staring at it. How I told her it was pretty, and she said it was the sleeping powder of Ole Lukøje, but that if little girls had any of it, they would get carried away to the land of eternal sleep, so I should never touch it…."

Tohko was utterly pale and looked as if she might collapse at any moment. A profound despair was in her eyes.

"I-I told him. I was trying to act like a big sister…I told him about how mom had the sleeping powder of Ole Lukøje and how the key to the jewelry box with the bottle in it was hidden on the top shelf of her bookcase. I was scared, so all I did was look up at the shelves, but Ryuto—maybe he got a chair and peeked at it—he might have gotten the key and opened the jewelry box—"

*"Someone points at a shelf—and they tell me."*

*"The sleepin' powder of Ole Lukøje is up there—"*

The voice Ryuto had heard. It had belonged to Tohko. The finger pointing at the shelf had been hers, too.

173

"I-I told him, which means…"

It was painfully clear just how much Tohko blamed herself. I felt as if my chest would tear open also. But for Ryuto's sake, I had to reveal the truth.

"Ryuto was wearing a red sweater the morning of the accident, right?"

Tohko replied, forcing her voice out, "…Yes."

I thought so—a breath like a sigh escaped my lips.

"Ryuto told me that when Yui poured the poison out, her hand was white and silky, the sleeve of her sweater was dyed red like blood, and the poison cascaded down from it. That was Ryuto's own hand. I know that because Yui and Fumiharu had both dressed up to go to the wedding. Neither of them would be wearing a sweater."

The Christmas photo had probably shown Ryuto in a red sweater. When he saw that, Ryuto had realized, too.

That the hand pouring out the poison had been his own—

"He must have gotten up on a chair or something in the moment that Fumiharu took his eyes off him and put the poison into their coffee. The night before, Yui had had a fight with Fumiharu, and she'd seemed tired the next morning. If she had a fun dream, maybe she would cheer up. Maybe that's how he thought of it."

And then that memory had turned into a memory from Takumi Suwa, and the one who brewed the coffee changed from Fumiharu to Yui, and Ryuto convinced himself that Yui was the one who'd added the poison. That Takumi had given her the poison in order to save her from her suffering.

And yet after he'd seen the photo album and learned that wasn't true, he searched the drawers and found the empty bottle—

And then he'd been so crushed that he tried walking into death.

Maybe the reason Ryuto believed he was a reincarnation was so that he could transfer the crime he'd committed onto Takumi and try to forget about it. That unconscious panic might have provoked him into all the violent acts he'd committed up till now.

Kanako, too, wore a flabbergasted look as she murmured, "Yui talked about Ole Lukøje's poison. At the time it sounded like a snide remark directed at me, but...when I heard that they'd been in an accident under unusual circumstances, I thought Yui really had had poison and that she really had used it. I never thought Ryuto..."

Her hands still firmly clasped together, Tohko's head drooped. Kanako's expression was bleak and heavy, too.

"Yui didn't commit suicide because she was afraid you were going to steal Fumiharu from her. And she didn't do it because she hated you, either."

Kanako looked at me. The transformation of her rage filled her eyes with sorrow that had no outlet, and she murmured, reproachful, "How do you know that?"

"Because Tohko told me about the story like manna that Yui dreamed of writing someday."

Tohko looked at me frailly.

"She said that Yui always talked about it...a sweet, pure story that would fill an empty stomach like the white sustenance God rained down from heaven. Tohko and Fumiharu were both filled up by the meals Yui wrote for them. The empty one was you, Kanako. Yui wished she could write a story for you."

Kanako moaned.

"That's just some imagination you're trotting out."

"Yes, that's true. But Tohko and Ryuto both tried to make me write that novel. Since something I wrote was like Yui's stories, they tried to make me write in Yui's place. Ryuto wasn't choosy about his methods. He even tried to commit a crime. For your sake, he was desperate."

I remembered Ryuto crying outside the gate of my house and a digging pain ran through me. I couldn't forgive Ryuto for his actions. But he'd been suffering, too. He'd wanted to rescue someone important to him.

Kanako let out a mournful scream.

"But you won't write ever again! You quit being an author! Yui did, too; once she married Amano, she threw away her dream of being an author! She never showed me anything ever again. Everything Yui wrote belonged to Amano after that! I was Yui's reader until she met Amano! She found a new reader, and she didn't need me anymore!"

The cascade of feelings that had lost any other outlet came at me with a groan.

The walls had broken down; the penned-in emotions surged up and raged.

At last Kanako was speaking fragments of truth.

For nine whole years—no, ever since Yui and Fumiharu met, Kanako had held the pain of being betrayed in her heart.

Her face twisted fiercely and she cried out unselfconsciously. It mirrored the way I'd acted when I learned of Tohko's lies and mirrored the way Miu had reproached me in the blizzard on the roof. At last, I understood.

Kanako was a reader betrayed by her author.

That's why she'd become an author and taken her revenge. No story would ever be told for her again. All she could do was tell it herself. All she could do was continue writing to assuage her hunger—

"I never liked the novels Yui wrote in the first place. She started clinging to me obnoxiously in middle school and posing as my best friend—saying things like she wished we could be together forever, without even a hint of shame. Making me read the sloppy stories she'd written—

"She'd told me that she loved me more than anyone, and yet the day when she first brought a manuscript to Amano, she purposely came to my house, her face bright red, and exhausted me with stories of how great he was. After that, every time she saw me all she talked about was Amano!

"She used the excuse of having him look at a manuscript, but all she wanted was to see him.

"He was the same way! There was no commercial value whatsoever in the fluffy fairy tales Yui wrote, and yet he kept seeing her. Yui was his goal all along!"

Kanako's eyes flashed with hatred. The rawness of it took my voice away. It was like a storm howling in the room.

"He told Yui he wanted her to become his author exclusively, and yet I would be writing something while beside me that man would kick back and eat Ogai Mori or Tolstoy. He didn't tell Yui that he was seeing me. And yet she married him and even got pregnant. She told me about it ecstatically. She was flaunting her happiness at me!"

"...And because you couldn't forgive her for that, you committed an indiscretion with Fumiharu."

Kanako's lips twisted into a smirk.

The way they had when she told me the address of the temple where Yui's grave was.

The way they had when she'd muttered that she wished Tohko would never come back.

With a look that held intense hatred.

"No. I wanted to teach Yui a lesson. That the happiness she treasured so much was just like the stories she wrote—nothing more than a phantom. That her husband was the worst kind of man, one who'd had an affair with another woman while his wife was pregnant."

Tohko lowered her eyes, looking like she was on the verge of tears.

I recalled how she had told stories about her parents with a smile, and I, too, felt it grow difficult to breathe.

In the picture, Fumiharu and Yui had looked so happy together, though. Why had Fumiharu transgressed with Kanako?

"I was at the Kanazawa Hotel to get material, and when I called Amano there, he left Yui and came running.

"I asked him, am I your author or is Yui?

"I told him that if he went back to Yui that night, I would never write again."

Was Kanako the author for Fumiharu Amano, or was it Yui?

One was Fumiharu's embodiment of the ideal; the other was indispensable everyday life.

Which of the two opposite women did Fumiharu love more deeply?

"Amano didn't go home. 'If it will feed your writing...' He smiled and then betrayed Yui."

What kind of smile had Fumiharu worn that night?

A bitter smile? A gentle smile? A melancholy smile? A smile of resolve? A smile of despair?

Then Kanako's voice grew slightly quieter, and I saw her eyes were lowered. I thought revenge might not be the only reason Kanako had had a romantic relationship with Fumiharu.

I didn't know if it was what you would call love between most men and women. I was pretty sure it wasn't.

Even so, hadn't there been a bond between Kanako the author and Fumiharu the editor that couldn't be measured by sensibility? Fumiharu was the man she loathed who'd taken her beloved best friend from her, but at the same time he understood her better than anyone.

*"If it will feed your writing…"*

With what emotions had Fumiharu said those words?
With what emotions had Kanako heard him?
And with what thoughts had Yui waited for Fumiharu to return?
The hatred faded from Kanako's eyes and a heartbreaking sorrow came into them.
"…That was the night Yui miscarried. And she fled into an imaginary world.
"She was convinced the child she'd lost was still inside her. She would say such things… 'If we have a girl, we're going to name her Tohko after *The Legends of Tono*… Oh, why can't she be born soon?' All while stroking her belly joyously."
Yui, her heart broken by the loss of the baby she should have had.
How deeply had Kanako tasted of despair and regret, seeing her best friend talking so happily?
Tohko looked closer to tears than ever and clutched at her skirt.
Ironically, in place of the life that was lost, Kanako had fostered a new life inside her.
"I had no need of a child. Something like that would only get in the way. So I foisted it off on Yui. Yui believed she'd given birth to it herself."
The words she spat out were colored by a pinching sadness.
Kanako turned her eyes away, as if afraid of letting us see into her heart. It made her look small and frail.

"Yui's spirit was weak. She couldn't deal with the harshness of reality. She rewrote reality and went on with her life in a happy dream world. Fearing meanwhile that her dream would shatter…

"The books she wrote were like that, too, that child. Sweet and pretty, overflowing with a sense of goodness, with only good people in them and not at all realistic."

As Kanako continued whispering brokenly, like cold rain falling, Tohko watched her without a sound.

The person who was her birth mother and also the best friend of the mother who raised her—

Aunt Kanako is a good, kind person. Tohko had said that to me cheerfully, and now—

Her eyes were wet, as if she was more concerned about Kanako's pain than her own.

And so I spoke up.

"But you loved those stories of Yui's, didn't you? That's why you couldn't forgive her for not letting you read them anymore and why you felt betrayed."


Love and hatred were separated by the space of a single sheet of paper.


Ryuto had said it all the time, too: you can hate someone because you love them.

You can keep loving someone because you hate them.

Because hatred lasts longer and more powerfully than love.

All along Ryuto's eyes had been on Kanako, who loved Yui despite her hatred.

Burning for that almost crazed obsession to be directed onto him.

"I won't be confused by your lies anymore," I told Kanako with feelings that made my heart tremble. "You're the one who never tried to see the truth and rewrote reality, Kanako."

Kanako fixed her gaze on me with irritation. I looked right back into it.

"If you're saying you didn't want a child and that's why you pushed her off on Yui, then why did you bother giving birth with Yui's name? Even now you're pretending that you don't still love Yui. The way you wrote in *The Immoral Passage*, where there was nothing but hatred between Arisa and Yuiko.

"And that's not all. You even forged a letter to make people think that Yui was a two-faced, mean-spirited woman that was jealous of you."

Tohko caught her breath with a gasp. "Konoha, you...read that letter?"

"I'm sorry."

When I'd apologized for looking at the photos in the album, Tohko must have suspected as much. An ambiguous expression came over her face—not terribly surprised, just troubled.

On the other hand, Kanako had apparently also figured out which letter I'd read. Her gaze became that much harsher.

"The date on the letter was three days before the accident. But that was a lie you created. You wrote that letter after Yui and Fumiharu had died."

"What proof do you have for saying something like that? I can tell you Yui sent me that letter before she died. Because I couldn't stand her hiding her jealousy of me and smiling so congenially at me."

"Are you lying again? In the letter, you mentioned that Yui secretly had poison. As if you had found out where it was hidden and seen it for yourself. As if you were using it to threaten Yui. 'Are you going to put it in my food?' you'd ask smirkingly. But!" I shouted sharply.

181

The scene Ryuto had described rose into my mind accompanied by a smoldering heat. The black coffee swirling in a vortex. The silver grains pouring in smoothly.

"You might have known that Yui had the poison. *But you didn't know what form it was in.* Isn't that right? Otherwise you never would have written that she was going to 'poison my food.' People usually use liquids for that."

Kanako's face tensed.

"The fairy of sleep, old man Ole Lukøje who drips milk into children's eyes to make them sleep. You heard Yui talk about Ole Lukøje and got the impression that the poison was a liquid. But *it was actually powder! Tohko talked about how her mother had sleeping powder.* Why would you go to the trouble of writing in the letter about poison you had never seen, but pretend that you had seen it? Don't you think that's strange?"

As Kanako glowered at me with flashing eyes, her lips trembled ever so slightly. But they produced no response.

I turned to Tohko and asked, "Where was the letter, Tohko?"

Tohko probably knew, too. She answered quietly, her face sad, "It was stuck inside my mom's photo album."

"How old were you when you read it?"

"...After they died, we were going through their things. I read it then..."

I turned back to Kanako.

"You put it into the photo album on purpose *to make Tohko read it.*

"When Madeleine burned all of Gide's letters and threw them out, Gide despaired that he'd lost the best parts of himself, but for you it was the opposite. You hid the best parts and put the worst parts into a letter and exposed them!"

"That's enough!" Kanako shouted. "What possible benefit would there be in me doing something like that?!"

"You had to do it in order to protect your heart. Because you'd committed a sin against your beloved best friend."

"A sin?"

"Yes, because *you're the one* who killed Yui—"

At that, Kanako sucked in a breath. Her eyes opened wide and she looked astounded.

"At least, that's what you thought. That you had cornered Yui and driven her to her death. Every time Yui turned an uneasy look on you, you couldn't help but remember your sin—the sin of your indiscretion with Yui's husband, Fumiharu—the sin of causing Yui's child to die."

Maybe she'd been with Takumi Suwa and had Ryuto in order to reassure Yui.

I have no intention of stealing your husband or child.

Maybe she wanted to show Yui that she had a lover and a child of her own. The young man who consorted with countless women, the plaything, had been to cover her tracks, a convenient match for Kanako.

When I thought of how Ryuto must have felt, still caring for Kanako as he did, it was as if my chest were being carved out.

But when I considered that Kanako could have atoned for her sin in no other way, my heart hurt even more.

What a lonely, awkward woman she was. Kanako was lacking somehow as a person. I was sure Yui was the one who had filled in that empty spot.

"*Immoral Passage* was the confession of your sin and the short story sequel was your wish. The doll Toco grows up and kills Arisa. You thought Toco *had* to hate her, didn't you?"

Kanako fixed flaming eyes on me. Tohko was watching over us worriedly. I continued speaking.

"There was no way you could have loved Tohko! Because she was the proof that you had betrayed your best friend—your

183

beloved Madeleine. So you ignored her, kept her at a distance, and wrote that letter trying to make her hate you! You treated Tohko like a nonexistent child! And then you kept yourself alone and went through the narrow gate! Yui wasn't the weak-spirited one—it was you!"

Kanako was shaking with anger. Her eyes were bloodshot, she was grinding her teeth, and her shoulders were rising and falling as if she had trouble breathing.

Her face was crumbling bit by bit. She began to look crestfallen, her eyes tearing up, transforming into a picture of sorrow.

I was sure that what I had said wasn't the whole story.

People's hearts were complex and chaotic, and love and hatred got muddled together and there was no showing the shape of it clearly.

Why had Kanako kept Tohko close at hand? Why had she ignored her? Because she loved her or because she hated her? Kanako herself probably didn't even know the truth.

If she was nearby, even if it was more painful than words could say, at least she wouldn't be able to go away. So Kanako tried to hate her. Tried to be hated. Hating, hating, being hated, being hated—even so, their tie by blood was one thing she couldn't deny.

The same blood as hers was unquestionably flowing inside the young girl in front of her. Her eyes, her lips, the lines of her face proved that.

And yet her smile and mannerisms were exactly like those of the person she loved, whom she had no hope of ever seeing again. She spoke to her with the same inflections and gave her the same smile.

No matter how she pushed and pushed at her, her eyes were fixed on Kanako unflaggingly and she brought her love.

\*　　\*　　\*

Exactly the way she was when I met her—

For Kanako, it had been the torment of hell.

Being loved by a person she couldn't be allowed to love and trying never to love her.

Kanako had been suffering so much since losing Yui that she couldn't stop herself from rewriting reality completely. She had been crushed, like Gide when he lost Madeleine.

*"Everything has faded and lost its luster."*

*"I no longer know for what reason I would go on living…"*

Kanako's irreplaceable Madeleine.

Something joyous and torturous.

She had loved her, had hated her that much.

Kanako dug the fingers of one hand into her bangs and whispered in a ragged, exhausted voice, "Get out of here! Let me be alone! Get away from me."

"…Are you running away?" I asked quietly, and she looked at me with a faintly bitter face.

"Are you saying you didn't run away, Miss Miu Inoue?"

A sharp shot went through my chest.

"Your writing…is very similar to Yui's. You only see nice things. You're blind to people's evil intentions and only believe in good. You love superficial words like *dreams* and *hope* and *trust* and *thoughtfulness*, and you write endlessly about things that make you feel good, and that's it. The only reason you won the prize is because your fourteen-year-old feelings and writing style just happened to match the theme and it gave a better effect than we'd anticipated. That story…was like a miracle. But even if you could win the prize, you're not the type that could be an author.

Just like Yui. Quivering in the face of ugly reality, unable to look at the darkness in the soul, you break. You flee into a happy dream."

*"You could never be an author."*

I remembered being told that frigidly in the hotel lobby.

I have no intention of being an author. I'm not going to *be* an author!

The way I'd desperately defended myself in my heart while standing perfectly still and silent.

How I had felt an almost dizzying sense of dread for her, whom everyone acknowledged as an author.

I was no match for her. Before this person, I could only lower my head and shrink in on myself.

But it was different now.

"Like you said, I've done nothing but run this whole time. From becoming an author and from other people."

I'd tortured Miu, not realizing her true feelings. After Miu jumped off the roof, I secluded myself in my room and swore, weeping, that I would never write another novel.

Even after starting high school, I'd been a cowardly child who had thought only of crafting an exterior and living in peace.

"But now there's something I want to tell you, the author, and I'm not going to run.

"The novel you wrote is so perfected that my novel doesn't even compare to it. The style and composition were both incredible. But I can't sympathize with the main character Arisa. It's the same with you."

I looked Kanako in the eyes and told her my honest feelings. I could feel Tohko's gaze on my cheek.

"You're like Alissa when she left Jerome, thinking that there's only one path.

"Nothing but the path that leads to supremacy means anything, and naive authors who rely on family or friends can't survive. Isn't that a narrow view? Alissa's noble self-seclusion was haughty and pure. But it was also something selfish that didn't consider Jerome's feelings. Do you intend to cast aside your family and the people who care about you and go through the narrow gate all alone?"

Kanako answered coldly, "I can't change the way I live. I've walked alone this far."

"Alone? *That's exactly how you've always rewritten the story! To suit yourself!* You wrote in your novel that you were the one who killed Fumiharu, who killed Yui, who killed the baby Toco, and you wrote a story where the doll Toco hated you and killed you. You put a letter that made it seem like you and Yui hated each other into Yui's photo album in order to make Tohko read it."

Kanako was silent, wearing a stubborn expression. A steely light was in her eyes.

I wanted to get it across to this woman.

What I had seen in my despair. The truth I had grasped there.

"I suppose that for you, the act of writing a novel means telling the ugly truth exactly as it happened.

"But if there's an ugly truth, a beautiful truth must exist, too. Stories aren't purely ugly. They're not purely tragic or sad, either. There are tender things and beautiful things in there. The way I turned away from pain and ugliness, you, Kanako, didn't try to see kindness or hope. You denied it and rewrote it. I'm a coward, but you're arrogant!"

"What would a child like you know?"

Her cold voice struck my ears.

"Yes, I'm a child. But I won't be a child forever! Someone educated me. They taught me a way to shine the light of imagination on dark reality and change the world—"

My heart was thrumming and my head was getting hot.

Yes, the person at my side, who was watching me with a prayer in her eyes—Tohko had taught me that.

Each time I'd been hit squarely by a blow and struck down, the book girl had held my hand and helped me to stand. She had changed the hope hiding in the dark world into shining words and told them to me.

On the roof at the beginning of summer, at the church in the middle of the night, at the shadowy estate, on the stage being watched by spectators, in the moonlit factory, below the starry sky glinting in the ceiling!

*"What is true happiness?"*

*"So perhaps the truly important thing is not that you get hold of something, but that you keep searching for it."*

*If you open the cover of a book, you'll encounter someone's imagination there.*

*"Lift your head and try looking at the sky! In this world, there are as many books and as much imagination as there are stars in the sky!"*

"An author doesn't simply present you with reality. They should be able to light a spark in it and imagine a new story! In *Strait Is the Gate*, Alissa is torn between Jerome and God. God is the ideal she must pursue, the thing she cannot touch in a high, faraway place. In order to behold it, she must go on alone—

"The same way that you said an author must be someone that goes through the narrow gate alone, Alissa cast everything aside and passed from the narrow gate. But does *Strait Is the Gate* make us cast everything aside to enter?"

I stood taller and declared, "I don't think so!"

Tohko's eyes widened.

"If you enter it with lots of things you've gained over time in your heart, there will be no reason to fear even a dark, narrow path. With the power of imagination, you can illuminate the dark path.

"Maybe that's just me being seventeen and not understanding anything. Maybe what you said was right. Maybe the pitch-dark path goes on interminably beyond the gate and a despair you can't possibly imagine lies in wait for you there.

"But I'm seventeen and I read *Strait Is the Gate*, and that's how I felt.

"This is the truth for me right now that I thought about and took hold of at seventeen!"

A smile like violets was spreading across Tohko's lips and eyes.

The warm smile that had always shone a light on my heart—

"Are you saying you're going to write a novel just to show me? In Yui's place?" Kanako asked me, getting annoyed.

I smiled abruptly.

"No."

I had finally reached it.

I had finally gotten here.

With that soft, satisfied feeling, I said, "I'm not the one who's going to write Yui's story. That's you, Kanako."

Surprise came over Kanako's face.

"What are you talking about?"

"Yui already left behind a story for you. You just haven't realized it."

Kanako's eyebrows hiked up, and in a stringent voice she said, "There wasn't even a diary in Yui's things, let alone a story. If you're talking about the letters you saw, you've guessed wrong. Yui isn't the one who wrote those."

Tohko's expression wilted.

The letters that had fallen from the pale violet box and scattered—who had written those? Who had torn them up? I had a realization.

The one who'd written them was Tohko.

She must have been calling out to Kanako with her mother's feelings.

After I'd left the condo, Kanako had gone back to the house and checked what the letters said. She realized that it wasn't something Yui had written, and she must have been in transports of rage and torn them up.

That night, how had Tohko felt when she got home and had to pick up the fragments of the letters scattered around the room? When I thought about it, it made my chest squeeze tight.

"Those false letters?! Are you trying to trick me, telling me that's Yui's story?"

"I'm not. Yui's story isn't something written down in a letter. It's something that's been at your side this whole time."

Kanako knit her brows.

"It's right in front of you, right now. It's worried about you. It's wishing it could talk with you."

Kanako's gaze turned slowly toward Tohko, who stood beside me.

She fixed her eyes on the book girl with her braids, standing there desolately, and she gasped as if she'd been shot through the heart.

Her face still tense as she looked at Tohko, I told her, "The story Yui left for you is Tohko."

A fresh surprise came over Kanako's face.

"Tohko would tell me exuberantly that you're a good, kind person.

No matter how harsh the treatment she got from you, she adored you.

"Those feelings are something she inherited from Yui. Yui loved you and always talked about you, so Tohko inevitably started to love you, too. Yui gave her love for you to Tohko. The story like manna that Yui spent her entire life writing was inside Tohko."

The white, pure sustenance fluttering down from God in heaven.

A sweet miracle gently filling an empty spirit.

It was the stories without count that Tohko had poured into our hearts until now.

With a sunny, kind voice, with clear, intelligent eyes—

Tohko had been hurt, too, in fact. She'd spent her days not being loved by someone she loved in a wish that might never be granted.

But in the midst of it, Tohko hadn't stopped turning the pages. She trusted in hope, trusted in the future, and kept turning to the next page.

She had gently taken the hands of people curled up in despair and what the book girl with her braids told them wasn't a Pollyanna dream. They were the heartwarming, encouraging words of a girl who knew of darkness and knew of pain, and who was trying to overcome them.

*"Try imagining something happy, that the future is bright and wonderful!"*

*"After you wake up from a beautiful dream, the story stays in your heart."*

*　　*　　*

Surely that was something that her mother Yui had entrusted to her.

Something that Tohko was trying to pass on to Kanako.

Kanako was looking at her with a rigid expression. Conflict and thirst came into her eyes.

Tohko was looking back at Kanako with an earnest gaze.

After the passage of long years, the mother and daughter linked by blood were finally looking at each other. Now was the moment to pass on her mother's story, the story Tohko held in her heart.

"Kanako, I'm not the one who's going to complete Yui's story; you are. Please accept the story that was prepared for you."

That night in the planetarium, Tohko had passed the baton to me. She had looked at me and smiled, as if to say, "From now on, it's on your turn," and then she'd turned me toward Miu and let me give an important confession.

This time I would give the baton to Tohko—

When I squeezed her hand, Tohko flinched terribly and looked over at me.

She was confused, and still holding her hand, filling my words with my wish, I said sunnily, "All right, Kanako. If anyone can interpret the story Yui entrusted to Tohko, picture it, and write it down, it's you. Because you're an author."

Kanako's shoulders shook feebly. The hunger and thirst that had come into her eyes had grown so great she couldn't hide them anymore.

I looked at Tohko with a smile. Tohko's eyes were round. When I slowly guided the hand I held toward Kanako, a smile touched her lips. It spread steadily and became an overflowing smile.

I nodded, as if giving her the signal. Tohko nodded, too, then pulled her hand from mine and walked toward Kanako. Then, a smile still on her face, she started talking to her gently.

"Aunt Kanako…the reason I call you 'aunt' is because my mom told me to call you that. She told me, 'An aunt is like a second mother, and Kana is another mother for you, Tohko.'"

A shock ran over Kanako's face and it twisted as if it might shatter.

"My mom realized at some point that you were the one who'd given birth to me. So she was trying to tell me that you were my real mother. When I woke up at night, she would often be gazing at a purple bottle and talking to herself. She was saying, 'I'm sorry, Kana.'"

Kanako's face was breaking down steadily. Her lips trembled and her face was falling.

Yui hadn't been a weak person secluding herself in a dream world.

It may have been that way at first, but she realized the truth on her own. She had suffered, but even so she'd hidden that fact and smiled warmly.

And she had poured so much of her love for Kanako into Tohko.

For the day when she would eventually give Tohko back to her.

She was someone who'd had that strength.

"The letters I wrote under my mom's name weren't a lie. They were all things I'd seen and things my mom had told me. She enjoyed telling stories about you, flipping through the photo album, more than anything else. She would always tell me that you were her best friend, that she'd loved you ever since the first time she met you, and that she'd wanted to be with you."

Tohko wove her words kindly, sweetly.

Pure manna was falling from the sky, glittering white.

"My mom was upset, thinking that she'd stolen your happiness from you, Aunt Kanako. The reason she looked at you uneasily wasn't out of jealousy. It's because she was worried about you."

Kanako listened to Tohko's voice, trembling. Her red, swollen eyes were focused, trying to interpret the story left to her by the person she'd loved.

"About two weeks before she died, my mom held me in her arms and cried. That day she told me."

Tohko's eyes were faintly touched with tears, too.

But still smiling softly, her voice penetratingly kind—the girl who looked like Kanako told her with Yui's voice and gaze, "I wish Kana could realize that there are people who love her.

"I wish she could realize how little Ryu feels.

"I wish she would let him call her 'mom.'"

The things Yui had wanted to tell her.

That Kanako wasn't alone.

That there were people who loved her.

That, if only she would realize it, she could have a family—

Tohko stretched a hand out toward Kanako. A slip of pale pink paper like a cherry blossom petal rested in the palm of her open hand. It was the one scrap of the letter that Tohko had picked up.

*"Dear Kana"*

It was written in a gentle hand.

Tohko's eyes were soft and clear as she gazed at Kanako, too.

Sparks of turmoil came over Kanako's face. Her hand was shaking as she reached out toward Tohko's. Their hands overlapped, and a whisper slipped from Kanako's lips, sounding as if it had been wrung out of her.

"…Tohko."

Tohko looked like she was about to break into tears. And then she smiled, like a flower bathed in light.

Kanako's face was taut, as if she was desperately trying to contain the sway of her intense emotions.

But when Kanako held the infant Tohko in her arms for the first time, she had smiled with joy.

She brought her face close to Tohko's cheek and called her "Tohko."

She'd rejoiced with all her heart at Tohko's birth.

Kanako softly squeezed the slip of paper in Tohko's palm. She brought it tenderly to her chest, and with a cool face she whispered, "...Where is Ryuto's hospital?"

Those were the words of a beginning for Kanako.

——⟫◆⟪——

I wanted to write for you, Kana.

You've watched Tohko eat the stories I wrote, haven't you?

I've wanted to give you your wish for a long time.

I've wanted to let you be full.

I've wanted to give you lots and lots of sweet, sweet manna, like pure white snow that God rains down from the sky.

Be nice to Ryu, okay, Kana?

Listen to what he tells you. Let him call you mom.

Ryu loves you, Kana.

Tohko and I will always love you, too, Kana.

I'm not going to use the sleeping powder of Ole Lukøje.

I'll be waiting with Tohko when the time comes that you finish your long journey and come back from that gate to us.

I'll open my arms wide for you and smile.

Please God, let Kana be the happiest person in the world.

## Chapter 8—The Scribe Who Faced God

Dawn was breaking when Ryuto woke up.

The second he saw Kanako, his face twisted up in disbelief and tears filled his eyes.

"…Mom."

He called to her, as if to confirm that he could say it, and then he sobbed fat tears, like a little child.

Kanako only murmured brusquely, "…Today was my deadline. What a troublesome boy."

When she heard that, Tohko looked like she might indeed cry, and then she smiled.

Apparently Ryuto had been in real danger briefly, and he ended up being hospitalized for a fair amount of time.

Maki had deftly pulled some strings with the police on the Takeda situation apparently. When I went to visit Ryuto after school, Takeda was there.

Sitting on a chair beside his bed, leaning back against Ryuto's chest, her eyes were closed peacefully. Ryuto was tenderly stroking her fluffy hair.

"…Thanks for tryin' to kill me."

"I killed the Takumi that was inside you, Ryu. All that's here now is Ryu, who's all for me. You can't cheat on me anymore. If you start to like anyone but me, I'll kill you and then I'll die, too."

Takeda turned her face toward Ryuto.

I saw their lips slowly approach each other, and I quickly quieted my footsteps and snuck out of the room.

I understood how they felt, but I couldn't burst in on their tender moment.

Still carrying the flowers I'd brought for my visit, I was wearing a blush in the hallway when Maki called out to me.

"Well, well, did you get hit with the dopey couple?"

"Um...did you come to visit Ryuto, too?"

"You know, just to check up on him. There was a line of girls here before, and that kid chased off every last one of them. You missed something incredible."

"I did?"

Her sensual lips pulled up with pleasure.

"She stood in front of the room, put a box cutter against her throat, and told them, 'If you come one step closer, I'll cut myself. Ryu's my boyfriend, so please don't go near him.'

"Since she said it in a deadpan with that expressionless doll-face, it scared everyone and they all left."

My heart was rushing.

*What are you thinking, Takeda—?!* It terrified me how she seemed like she really could just go *slice.* I was sure everyone had sensed that it wasn't a threat and it had given them a shudder.

"Ryuto finally got his hands on his ideal woman."

She said it with a breezy expression, then put her hands to her stomach with a candid look on her face.

I remembered that even now Ryuto's child was in there.

What would Maki do next?

My heart squeezed tight, but there was no shadow over Maki's face.

"I can't kill someone or chain them up just because I love them.

"So I couldn't have been Ryuto's only lover. But I will have the baby. It'll probably throw Grandpa and the rest of them into conniptions, but it's not as if I care. Actually, I can't wait. Because this child is a symbol of my freedom, from a boy that I liked by my own choice!"

Her hand still resting on her stomach, she lifted her face and made her declaration with a regal smile.

The sight of her like that was incredibly brilliant and powerful.

Maki would probably love the child she bore with all of her heart.

She would probably tell it the same thing she was telling me now.

With her chest thrown out brazenly, proudly.

*"You are the child of a man I loved."*

"Could I have those flowers?"

"Go ahead."

I held the cute bouquet of tulips and baby's breath in a riot of spring colors out to her reverently, and Maki accepted it happily.

"Heh-heh. Thanks."

When I left the hospital, a gentle dusk colored everything outside.

Clouds shining faintly peach floated in a sky the color of water. Through them shone straight beams of light, like a stairway climbing to the heavens.

A golden hour both warm and holy.

A gentle, melancholy backdrop in which love, sadness, hatred, and hope had melted together and been strained out like amber-colored consommé.

In the shallow light, Tohko's figure appeared and I heard her clear voice.

198

*     *     *

*"Konoha."*

In front of a rippling curtain, she looked at me and smiled like a violet.

*"Hey, do you know what an improv story is? You write a story using three keywords."*

A pure white piece of paper. A mechanical pencil. A girl with braids from the next grade up tilting her head teasingly and clicking a silver stopwatch.

The things she had given to me.

The book club after school, the aroma of old books, mounds of books. The sound of pages turning.

A desk with an uneven surface the color of dark tea, a fold-up chair beside a window.

Dust dancing in the light.

A soft smile. A bright voice expounding on something. A torrent of glittering words.

The sun sank, and in the glow before the world fell asleep, the images I'd seen up till now rose again in my mind. In every one, Tohko was there.

My heard pounded with a *thmp...*

Ever since making the proclamation to Kanako that beautiful stories existed, too, there had been something squirming impatiently inside my heart, trying to beat its wings.

A creature with huge wings was flying out of the deepest part of my body. It was the impulse to write these images down for posterity.

I want to write.

About this golden scene, warm and pure, that gathers desolation and kindness and love and everything into itself.
About the girl smiling within it.

I want to write.

About these feelings, so sweet and tender it makes my heart tremble.
I want to put it into words and tell people!

A shock bolted through my brain—as if something I hadn't been able to see up till now had suddenly been pointed out right in front of me and my field of view had opened up.

My skin itched almost electrically, my pulse quickened, my chest felt tight, my emotions were harried—before I realized it, I was running home, muttering, "I have to write, I have to write."

I have to write.

While this trembling, this impulse, stays in my soul.

I want to make notes about it. I want to express it. I want to share it.

Everything that's happened since I met Tohko.

The time that was like being inside a gentle sunset that had no comparison.

What kind of a person Tohko was. What she taught me. How we had spent our time.

The instant I returned home, I sat at my desk, opened my fifty-page notebook, and began to write rabidly with a mechanical pencil.

While I strung the letters together, moving the pencil so intently that I practically forgot where I was, I remembered the first time I'd written a novel.

How I had loved Miu so, so much that I could hardly bear it; how I had wanted to tell her more than anything; and how I had filled the lines of paper, my mind filled with thoughts of her. How my heart had pattered and felt like it might burst.

I had searched my heart and it turned into words, which embarrassed me but inevitably made me happy.

I want to write better! I want to share this more skillfully! How can I get it across? What words should I choose?

Through trial and error, the more I wrote, the more my heart fluttered and the more the pages I'd written in my notebook increased, which made me so, so happy.

Even though I had refused so thoroughly to write until now.

Even though I had thought writing was nothing but suffering.

Those days when I had spent the time writing with Miu in my thoughts, I really had had more fun than I could describe, stringing words together, adding sentences, and creating a story.

Like the trees stretching their supple, green branches toward the clear sky, the more I wrote, the more I'd felt as if my feelings were swelling toward infinity, as if I could go anywhere at all.

Of course, there were also times partway through when I got stuck. But I'd pondered it for all I was worth, and when I'd managed to break through it, it had made me even happier.

I want Miu to read this soon! I want her to be happy!

The way I'd felt back then reawakened vividly in my heart, my eyes, my fingertips.

Right now, in this moment, I was blissful, as if I was enfolded in absolutely pure light, the way I'd been unbearably happy when I was writing my novel in those days.

The way I'd felt Miu close by back then, now I felt Tohko's hand, her gaze, her breathing with all of my five senses—with all of my heart.

\*      \*      \*

*"Write a novel someday, okay? Let me read the story you write, okay?"*

The book girl had been drawing away, but now she was right in front of me, smiling purely.

*"I'm hungry, Konoha. Write me something, pleeeease."*

*"Yummm! It tastes like piping-hot steamed buns!"*

At some point, writing snacks for Tohko had become fun. I would fill the notebook paper, excited to think about how she would react.

In that tiny room dyed by the coming evening, I was an author and Tohko was my reader. I knew well the contentment of writing and the joy of having someone to read it.

I couldn't write Yui's story.

But I would write my own! I wanted to finish it and give my answer to Tohko!

Because she was the one who'd been giving me the strength to write all along—

From then until graduation, I wrote continually at home and at school.

Maki told me that Tohko was coming to school even though her exams were still in front of her and was working as a model for her paintings.

"Tohko was the one who came and told me she wanted me to paint her. Even though she was incredibly angry that I was pregnant with Ryuto's baby. I'll draw with everything I've got, too. I plan to make it the best picture I've ever done."

She talked excitedly.

Maybe Tohko was trying to leave something behind, too.

She was supposedly coming to school, but she never showed herself at the book club or to me. I didn't go see her, either.

I just faced my notebook paper and kept on writing.

There wasn't enough time before graduation.

I had to make it.

Akutagawa didn't ask me about it.

He watched over me with an earnest gaze as I wrote in my notebook, even during lunch.

Kotobuki had been looking at me sadly.

Biting her lip, with eyes that seemed to ask, "Why are you writing the book you said you weren't going to write? Who are you writing it for?

"I thought you didn't want to write anything like that. Didn't you cry because you didn't want to write? So then why are you writing?"

Her tearful eyes that seemed to criticize me—I felt as if they were begging me, "Don't write!!" Each time, a gouging pain shot through me. My cheeks burned with Kotobuki's eyes on them, my throat closed up, and it was hard to breathe.

But I kept moving my pen.

I couldn't talk to Kotobuki right now.

I knew that when I finished writing this novel, I would have an answer.

It was on March 12 that I heard Tohko was having her secondary exam that day.

"She said they'd announce the results on the twenty-third. If Tohko gets in, you won't be able to see her the way you have up till now."

The name Maki told me was a school even farther north than her father's hometown.

Graduation was closing in with two more days to go.

And that day was also the fourteenth.

The day had come.

I put the three hundred and fifty pages I had stayed up all night to finish into an envelope, and I left the house.

I had conquered my sleepiness and my eyes were clear. Feeling the still slightly chilly breeze of early spring on my skin, I cut through a neighborhood and headed onto a major road.

Before I gave the manuscript to Tohko, I would talk to Kotobuki.

Apologize for everything that had happened, and then…

I saw Kotobuki standing in the place we used to meet and my breath caught.

She had a white peacoat on over her school uniform and hugged her schoolbag in her arms with her head bent.

"…Kotobuki."

When I called to her softly, her shoulders twitched and she raised her face; then she smiled feebly.

"Morning, Inoue…Today's the fourteenth, huh?"

"I'm sorry I didn't have time to get you anything in return for Valentine's Day."

"No, it's fine."

Still smiling, Kotobuki shook her head. Then she looked at the paper bag under my arm and her face grew sad.

"…You finished your novel, huh?"

"Yeah."

"…You're giving it to Tohko, right?"

"Kotobuki, I—"

"Tear that novel up."

She said it with a face on the verge of tears, and I gulped. I saw her face, and my throat closed up even more. My chest was being crushed in the grip of it.

"I'm sorry, I can't. And I can't be with you."

The eyes looking up at me were filling with tears.

"Yeah…I figured. You called me Kotobuki before. That was your answer, right?"

Pain pierced my throat. But I had to say it. All the way to the end and do it right.

"You did a lot to save me, Kotobuki, and I got courage from you. When you told me I didn't have to write anymore, I was so incredibly happy. Right then, I thought I wanted to be with you forever."

Kotobuki's face crumpled like tissue paper, and she shouted in a sharp voice, "But you wrote a novel!! You said you didn't want to, but then you wrote it!"

The tears had filled to the brim and spilled down her cheeks. Kotobuki scrubbed the tears away with one hand, but even so they welled up in fat bulbs, so she hung her head.

"I-I thought that if it was hurting you, then it was better not to write.

"But…that wasn't true, was it? I really wasn't the one who understood you best. It was Tohko. I was no good for you."

Desolation was welling up in me. I didn't know just how much Kotobuki's presence had helped me until then. And if Kotobuki hadn't been there when I'd thought Tohko had betrayed me, I wouldn't have been able to take it. I had truly felt tender toward her brusque way of talking and her awkward looks. I'd wanted to treasure her.

And yet I'd hurt her and made her cry.

*I'm sorry, Kotobuki.*

*And I'm sorry, Omi.*

"The scarf you gave me…I promised I would treasure it forever, but I lost it."

Her throat quivered and she sobbed as she spoke. The ground at her feet was wet with her falling tears.

"...Ngh, I have a request. Say my name just once—once is all I need."

Feeling as if my heart were being torn to bits, I said it.

"...Nanase."

Kotobuki lifted her face. She smiled awkwardly, her cheeks still soaked from her tears.

"Thank you...It's been my dream that you would call me by my name. It came true. Thank you. That makes me happy."

Her tears fell fast. She was smiling, but it didn't look anything like a smile.

"I'm going to go on ahead, okay? I'm sorry...can you stay here a little longer?"

Then she asked, "If Tohko goes far away and you can't see her anymore, would you let me be your girlfriend again?"

"I can't do that."

"Oh...um, I read *Strait Is the Gate*, too. That's...all I wanted to say. I don't know what it means. It's okay not knowing, though. I'll see you in class."

She spun around, then moved off quickly, rubbing at her face with one hand.

I stood there until her bobbing back disappeared around a corner.

Mori hit me. "You made Nanase look like an idiot! She's liked you this whole time!!"

In the corner of the empty hallway, Mori's eyes were bright red and full of tears.

The graduation ceremony started before I had any time to go to the third-year classrooms.

Tohko's name was called, and when I saw her mount the stage, my chest grew hot.

Swaying her long, thin braids, she accepted her diploma, bowed, and then turned around. She was smiling placidly.

When the ceremony ended, we had homeroom, and when that ended, school let out.

I hurried to Tohko's classroom with the brown envelope with the manuscript in it. All over the halls, I saw scenes of younger students handing the third-years bouquets or lamenting their separation.

But when I went to Tohko's classroom, someone in her class told me that she'd already left.

Could she be at the clubroom?

Panting, I opened the door to the book club in the western corner of the third floor. Tohko was standing in front of the window, looking at the view outside.

"Tohko?"

When I spoke, she gradually turned around.

She wore a placid smile, just as she had when I saw her on the stage. She held in her arms the tube with her diploma in it and several bouquets.

"Congratulations."

"Thanks. Although I still haven't decided what I'm going to do next, so I don't really feel like I've graduated."

"You said you would tell me if you got into college, right?"

"You're right. I'll come let you know."

We were only talking in an ordinary way, but my chest was filling with desolation.

"I was looking at the tree under this window just now."

"Which one...?"

I stood beside Tohko and looked down.

In the bright sunlight, a thick tree stood stretching out its branches. It was the tree Tohko had almost fallen out of when I was a first-year.

"Do you remember, Konoha? I was trying to climb the tree one morning and you passed by."

"How would I forget that? A normal president wouldn't be climbing trees first thing in the morning."

"I wasn't really trying to put a baby bird back in its nest."

*I wouldn't be right in the head if I believed an excuse like that.* I thought this, but I kept quiet.

"There's a trick where if you tie a ribbon around a tree branch at school without anyone seeing you, your wish is supposed to come true. So I wanted to tie a ribbon up, too. I got disappointed because I thought I'd failed when you saw me. But after I hung the ribbon up to dry in the clubroom, it disappeared, and then I found it tied around a branch of the tree."

"..."

"You had a scrape on your cheek that day."

"..."

"There was also a scrap of leaf stuck to the front of your uniform."

"I don't remember it that well," I said curtly, and Tohko stopped looking at the view, turned her face toward me, and smiled.

"Yeah...it's been more than a year. It's ancient history."

Her gaze was very kind and enfolding...wrenching my heart even more.

"Tohko, here."

I held out the heavy brown envelope in both hands.

"For graduating."

I looked Tohko straight in the eyes, packing my emotions into them.

"It's the novel I wrote. I'm giving it to you."

Tohko's face grew serious.

Then she looked like she was about to cry, and after that she slowly smiled.

"Thank you. I'll enjoy it."

She accepted the envelope and hugged it to her chest like a treasure, along with the tube and flowers.

"I'll take my time reading it once I get home."

The gentle gesture filled with affection made my chest grow hot.

"I'm sorry, I have to go now. I'm meeting Aunt Kanako. We're going to tell Ryuto about the graduation."

"Are things going well with Kanako?"

"Well…it's still hard for us to talk after all. But I'm sure it'll just take a little more time."

She probably thought that was fine. Tohko's tone was placid and tender.

Whenever Kanako wrote Yui's story, she would probably tell Tohko her true feelings through that.

Because I doubted she was the kind of person who could say it out loud.

Because even when she was with someone she loved, she was the kind of person who found it difficult even to smile. She could only say things through writing.

And so Kanako Sakurai would continue to be an author.

"Remember to come tell me if you get in."

"I will."

"If you don't, I'll think you flunked after all."

"It's fine. I'm confident."

Tohko puffed up her flat chest and smiled.

They would announce the results on March 23.

One week later and the passage of time felt slower. At the same time, I felt the urgency that there was only a little bit of March left.

When April came, I would be a third-year and Tohko would go north.

Though if by some chance she didn't pass, she might take a year off and come hang out in the clubroom between study sessions.

This was Tohko, who'd gotten hit with an F on her end-of-year tests. She might've bragged that she was confident, but the chances of flunking were way higher. But she said the secondary exam didn't have a math section, so who knew. She might've passed...

Either way, it wasn't as if I would never see her for the rest of my life.

And yet, while waiting for that day, my chest had been twisted up by anxiety.

And then the twenty-third arrived.

Since today was the ceremony for the last day of classes, people dispersed from the school building during the afternoon and the place became deserted.

I went to the book club room, sat in a chair, and waited for Tohko to come.

I wondered what time they would announce the results. No way she would have gone to the school itself to get them...I'd heard there were services that would check the results for you and let you know by telegram or e-mail, but had she done that?

Even when the hour came when club usually started, Tohko hadn't appeared.

Outside was a pleasant blue sky and the cherry blossoms were blooming earlier than in most years. When I'd first met Tohko, spring had come unusually late. A long, long winter had dragged on, and the cherry blossoms seemed like they would never bloom.

But this year spring was early.

While I gazed at the pleasant scenery, I grew sleepy.

Spring had the power to seduce people into sleep. My body grew warm and my eyelids were so heavy I couldn't fight them.

Thinking, *Just a quick nap…*, I put my face down on the uneven surface of the desk and closed my eyes.

If Tohko came, I was sure she would wake me up.

The sound of a page turning…

The sound of a gentle tearing…

The rustling sound of chewing…

I woke up to the familiar sounds I'd taken in over two years.

The inside of the room was dyed by the golden western sun.

Dressed in her school uniform and sitting with her feet pulled up on a fold-up chair next to the window, Tohko was tearing up the pages of a book and putting the pieces into her mouth. The chair was positioned at an angle, so she was hidden from the light streaming in, and I couldn't really make out her expression.

But the book on her lap had only the very last page left. And only one or two bites of that.

There was a *riiip* and the page became even smaller.

She slowly chewed and swallowed it, and her slender fingers reached for the final scrap.

A faint sound of a page tearing.

Slightly open lips.

A fragment of a word disappearing inside them.

When she'd swallowed it, Tohko turned her head toward me.

Her face was sad.

Even though she always looked so happy when she was eating books.

"You were awake…?"

"I just woke up."

"Oh."

Her eyes softened gently. That, too, made her look more grown-up than usual.

"…I finished the last of *Alt-Heidelberg*. It was so sweet and heartbreaking…incredibly delicious. Thank you for buying it."

I gaped when I saw that the very last page had been torn out of the book.

"I got into college."

"…Congratulations."

"I told you I'd do great on the real one."

I tried to say something, but the words caught in my throat.

She spoke the name of the university in Hokkaido that I'd predicted she would, and then Tohko opened the bag at her side and took out a heavy-looking brown envelope.

It was the manuscript I'd given her.

Why was it still around?

It had been more than a week.

Tohko gazed at me with an even more profoundly kind look than before and said in a gentle voice, "The novel you wrote for me…was succulent, and gentle, and absolutely wonderful! It was so melancholy it made my chest ache until I couldn't bear it, but after I finished reading it, I felt pure and warm…I'm sure it would taste so good if I ate it."

Anxiety stabbed into my heart.

My voice was hoarse. "…I want you to eat it. That's why I wrote it."

Tohko shook her head.

"I can't eat this story."

She set the pages down on the desk.

"It would be wrong to eat it."

"Why?"

She wasn't making any sense.

But she had always been beside me while I was writing her

snacks, pressuring me to hurry, hurry, hurry. When I held one out, she'd take it with a grin and a "Thaaaaank yooou" and knock it back with a crunch.

I pulled the pages out of the envelope and flipped through them. There was no sign that a single one of them had been touched. That meant—

"Take it to Mr. Sasaki, Konoha. That's what you need to do now."

My eyelids grew hot, and a burning lump filled my throat—and I begged.

"Why won't you eat it?!"

Sorrow colored Tohko's eyes. But a smile came over her face almost immediately, and like an older sister, she said, "Because I'm a book girl."

Her words were filled with a transparent decisiveness.

"I'm the daughter of Fumiharu Amano. My father loved my mother's food and he always looked so happy eating the things she wrote, but he would never eat the things Aunt Kanako wrote. He would say, 'I'm sure this would taste good if I ate it…but it would be wrong to eat this.' It was a story that had to be shared with everyone, so it would have been wrong for him to put it into his stomach."

My heart trembled.

My eyelids grew ever hotter.

"I don't—I don't understand that! I wrote it because I wanted you to eat it, Tohko!"

I had put the feelings I couldn't express very well out loud into my novel. I'd written for Tohko alone. And she'd even read it.

Had my feelings not come through to her even so?!

Had nothing gotten through to her?!

Why was she looking at me with those placid eyes? There was a handwritten manuscript right in front of her. Couldn't she tear in from the edges and eat with a crackle of paper like she always did?

"Please eat it! Please. I want you to eat it! I thought I was supposed to be your author!"

Tohko stood up, her face still gentle, then pulled my face close and hugged it in her arms.

She smelled like violets and my cheeks, ears, and eyelids were enfolded in a gentle warmth.

"Don't look so sad. C'mon, if you make such a sad face, I won't ever be able to have fun again, knowing that."

That was one of Kathie's lines from *Alt-Heidelberg*.

In the scene where the two part ways.

Tohko whispered in a placid, gentle voice, *"Ah, Karl Heinz, if you do that—if you do that, yes, if you do that, what shall I do?"*

The sound of Tohko's heart that I had once felt under my palm—I could hear it right against my ear.

*Thump, thump* . . . beating out a gentle pulse.

*"Youth is so beautiful and brief—"* she murmured sadly, then released her arms and pulled away from me.

She picked up her bag and stood up, then walked to the door.

I watched her with a despairing gaze, and then, as if to give me courage, she stopped and smiled. Then, in a tone she might use to teach something very important to a little child, she told me, "You can't be my author. You have to be an author for everyone. Because you're capable of that."

The door closed.

She was leaving.

I watched her go blankly, as if my soul had left my body.

*"You can't be my author."*

How could she say that now, after everything that had happened?

She was leaving.

But I'd written it for her.

She was leaving!

The emotions that shot up from inside me brought me to my feet, and I flew out of the room, chasing after Tohko.

The hall was empty already, and I didn't see her long braids or her delicate back anywhere.

I didn't even hear footsteps.

Feeling panicked, as if Tohko had disappeared into some unknown other world, I ran down the stairs and changed my shoes at the school's entrance.

The golden glow before night comes.

There was a girl moving through the school yard, swathed in the haze of that warm light, her long black braids dancing in the wind.

A petite back, a slender waist.

A rippling skirt.

White flower petals tumbling like flickering phantoms.

Even the scarf around her willowy neck was a brilliant white.

That scarf! It was mine! My scarf that Kotobuki said she'd lost!

I shouted so loud it tore at my throat. "Tohko!!"

In the gentle light and flower petals dancing in the wind, Tohko turned around.

Maybe it was because I was crying.

Her expression shifted until she looked like she was about to cry, too.

As fat tears rolled down my face, I ran up to Tohko, practically hurling myself at her, and hugged her slender body.

"This…isn't good-bye, right? We can still see each other whenever we want. Let me know your address when you find out what it's going to be. I'll write you a letter. I'll send you snacks every day. I could take a flight to Hokkaido, so that makes it closer than Iwate! You could take a train that stops at every station or an overnight bus, but who knows how long it would take you to travel, so I'll go to you! You wouldn't mind, right?"

"…You can't do that."

216

A kind voice whispered the words at my ear. They defied belief.

I lifted my face, and the image of Tohko smiling reflected in my wide, tear-filled eyes.

It was the face of someone who had already made her decision alone and was trying to move toward it.

"Nngh...why not?"

"I'm not sure, either. I can't explain it very well...and maybe I'm wrong. But I think this is how it has to be."

Like Alissa refusing the love of Jerome and going through the narrow gate alone—

As she looked at me with the eyes of a holy woman, filled with an affection greater than love, Tohko wiped away my tears with her fingers.

"Come on, Konoha...don't cry.

"From now on, even if you feel the tears coming, don't give in. If you do that, then the fact that you made all that effort and didn't cry will build your confidence."

As she wiped at the corners of my eyes, at my cheeks, at my lips with her sweet fingertips, she whispered slowly in a warm voice.

"Come on, don't cry...

"Throw out your chest...

"Smile...

"Take a good look, think...

"Stand up, and walk on your own."

As her almost tickling fingertips wiped the transparent beads from my cheeks, she peeked up at me from below. Her eyes were clear and peaceful, too.

"Promise me, Konoha. That you won't cry anymore. If I think that you're crying, I won't know what to do. I won't be able to be at your side anymore...I won't be able to wipe away your tears like this, either."

Tohko's fingers were so gentle, her eyes looking at me and her whisper of a voice, too; it was all so gentle—even though I told myself that it was wrong to cry, touched by her affection, my heart grew so full that the tears spilled out.

"Look, you're crying again."

Tohko's face fell, troubled.

I sobbed and said, "I'll make today the last time I cry. I won't cry again. I promise.

"I won't cry until the next time I see you, Tohko. I won't cry except when I'm with you! I promise!

"So please don't hold back if you want to cry, Tohko. When it gets so you want to cry more than you can believe, come see me. Please. Because next time I'll at least be strong enough to wipe away your tears."

I sniffled, tears coursing down my cheeks, but I knew I didn't sound convincing at all.

But these really would be my last tears.

I'm not going to cry anymore.

The smile disappeared from Tohko's face; fierce pain and sadness came into her eyes, and she looked like she might cry. But she smiled so prettily immediately after that it made my heart shake—

She unwound the scarf from her neck and put it around mine.

I was wrapped up in the warm texture of wool.

Cherry blossom petals swirling like snow fell in my hair and against my cheeks.

When Tohko tried to pull away from me, I grabbed her arm and pulled her back, and our lips met.

Tohko's were soft enough to melt away in, moist, and they tasted of salt.

Maybe that was the taste of my lips.

We came so close together that we could feel each other's heartbeats and the warmth of the other's body, and I tilted my head several times and closed my eyes—it felt like it went on a really long time.

When our paired lips parted, Tohko said, her eyes tearing up, "Meanie...that was my first time."

"Me too."

When I said that, my voice thick, Tohko's eyes filled even more.

Then, just like that, she smiled.

"Good-bye."

My first kiss became our good-bye kiss.

Tohko gently loosened her hand from mine.

The instant she turned her back, her long, thin braids fluttered up and caressed my cheek.

Tohko's retreating figure drew into the distance, as if she were melting away into the contented, golden hour before the arrival of night.

"Tohko!"

I shouted, feeling as if my heart was being torn apart, but Tohko didn't turn around again.

"Tohko! Tohko!!"

I called to her again and again through tears.

The name of the person who for two years had been at my side and, with all her heart, had enfolded me in her pale, kind hands—I yelled her precious name over and over.

Just as her name had promised, the "distant child" was steadily drawing farther away.

Before she passed through the school gate, her slender shoulders trembled just slightly. Maybe she was crying, too.

But she never stopped walking.

She stepped nobly through the gate and disappeared completely from my field of view, dimmed now by tears. The white scarf Tohko had wrapped around my throat swayed in the wind.

In the bright, burning world, covered in flower petals, I went back to the tiny room where the two of us had spent our time, bearing a deep sense of loss, as if I'd lost half of the heart beating in my chest.

An old hardcover was resting on the fold-up chair where Tohko had sat.

It was *Strait Is the Gate*.

When I turned back the cover, there was a dedication from Tohko's father. It was the book I'd seen on the shelf at Tohko's house. A pale violet envelope was stuck inside it.

I opened the envelope and read the long, long letter written on stationery of the same color.

Dear Konoha,

I don't think I'll be able to talk very well, so I'm writing you a letter.

Because I thought I would end up crying if I talked to you face-to-face.

There's something I never told you.

It must have bothered you, wondering how I knew about Miu Inoue's first draft.

I encountered the first novel you ever wrote the winter of my third year in middle school.

That day I needed to see Mr. Sasaki about something, so I went to the editing bureau of Summer's Breeze Publishing.

When I was little, my mom would take me there all the time to bring my dad a change of clothes, so it was a familiar place to me, full of memories.

I sat in a chair on the edge of the editors' floor and waited for Mr. Sasaki to be done with his work.

It was right when the manuscripts that had finished the initial selection for the new author prize were coming back in.

Cardboard boxes full of submissions were stacked all over.

They were picking from the ones that made it through the first round. They let me help while I waited for Mr. Sasaki. Your submission was in the discard pile.

I saw the title Like the Open Sky written in big, neat, handwritten letters and that was the start of it. My interest was hooked.

As I flipped casually through it and then continued to read on, I was pulled into Itsuki and Hatori's lush lives.

Before I realized it, I was immersed in it, oblivious to the world. Mr. Sasaki was surprised. I was plopped on the floor and turning through a rejected submission in utter silence.

The story you wrote was a lot like my mom's stories.

The way it was warm, and kind, and overflowing with love for someone.

As it went, it put me into a nostalgic, happy mood.

I especially loved the scene where Itsuki confesses her feelings to Hatori.

Maybe it wasn't great structurally, but Itsuki was adorable confessing so earnestly, and I imagined how very sweet this scene would taste if I ate it, how it had to be sour like lemon meringue pie and taste like happiness. I was enraptured.

Once I finished reading and let out a sigh, I held that manuscript out to Mr. Sasaki and I told him:

"Promise you'll read this.

"The technique might have some problems, but this is not a story you can reject—"

The sun had set and the room was cloaked in darkness. The letters receded into the shadows, and I couldn't make them out very well.

I turned on a light, then sat back down in the chair and continued reading, holding my breath.

One month later, when Mr. Sasaki told me that the story I'd pulled out of the rejection pile was still around in the final selections, I leaped for joy.

At the same time, I was so hopeful that my chest ached.

Because I knew Aunt Kanako was on the selection committee for the new author prize.

What would she feel when she read that story?

Would she think it resembled my mom's stories, the way I had?

I'd been writing letters to her for a long time.

Ever since my mom passed away, her heart had been closed.

Even though she was sadder than anyone at my mom's death, she couldn't say it out loud or show it in how she acted. She did things to deliberately sully her memories of my mom and hurt herself.

Even though I knew Aunt Kanako was suffering, I was incapable of doing anything.

If my mom were alive.

If she wrote the story of manna that she always talked about for Aunt Kanako.

Then Aunt Kanako wouldn't have needed to suffer.

If only I could take my mom's place.

With that thought, I took on my mom's emotions as I remembered the things she had told me and I went on writing letters to Aunt Kanako that would never be sent.

Dear Kana.

That's what I called her.

But she was steadily drawing away beyond the narrow gate, and no matter how much I called out to her, she wouldn't respond. She wouldn't even look at me.

It was as if she had shut her memories with my mom away deep in her heart and put a lock on them.

So I hoped that your story might touch her heart.

Your novel got chosen for the grand prize and became a book. Aunt Kanako didn't talk about it at home at all, but when I read her comments on the selection, hope came into my heart again.

If this kid put out a second book, maybe she would read that one, too.

If this kid kept on writing, maybe one day they'd be able to write the story of manna that my mom had wanted to write.

Maybe it would connect with Aunt Kanako's heart.

I saw your profile on your submission, so I knew that Miu Inoue was attending a middle school inside the city under the name Konoha Inoue.

Konoha—"leaves of the heart."

Konoha Inoue—

Was this kid a boy? A girl?

What kind of a person were they? What kind of wonderful stories would they write after this one?

Those were the selfish fantasies of a book girl.

But while I was daydreaming, thinking about all these things, my heart was oblivious and I was happy.

I was your very first fan, Konoha.

Tohko was your very first fan.

I recalled what Mr. Sasaki had told me.

And also what Ryuto had told me.

That if it weren't for Tohko Amano, Miu Inoue wouldn't exist.

The one who had discovered my run-of-the-mill story among so many submissions was Tohko. The one who'd liked my novel first, before anyone else, was Tohko.

224

Somewhere out there, a girl with braids who I had never met had read my story and been thinking about me. The thought of that filled my heart.

The two of us had been linked through novels since before we met.

When I quit writing, Tohko said in her letter that she'd been very, very glum.

And then she'd heard my name called at the welcoming ceremony the spring that she started her second year.

Konoha Inoue.

When the teacher read that name out, I thought my heart would jump out of my chest.

It could be them.

After the assembly, I went to the first-year classrooms, and when I found the name Konoha Inoue in the class rosters posted on the walls, I was truly thrilled.

It has to be! It's them!

That day you were sitting in your chair spacing out, not talking to anyone.

After I got home, I told Ryuto in a huge rush, "I met that kid! It's a boy!"

"Maybe he'll write again."

Oh, how wonderful that would be!

The light of a new hope caught in my heart, but Aunt Kanako had heard me talking.

"It's not going to happen. That boy could never be an author."

Her tone was cold and broke down my optimism. It made me think that she hated Miu Inoue, whom she'd never even met.

But despite her, I became more and more cheerful.

After all, the aunt who always ignored me had actually spoken to me!

It confirmed for me that Aunt Kanako had indeed felt your story was similar to my mom's. So I told her with a smile, "Then I'll make him an author! If Miu Inoue puts out another novel, you have to write a review."

It was a bet that I made without consulting anyone.

If I lost my gamble, I would disappear from Aunt Kanako's life. I realized that my existence tortured her. Even so, I wanted to share my mom's feelings with her someday.

Maybe that kid could do it. If he matured—!

I'll turn him into a true author.

I'll make him write another novel.

I made my decision with a joy that had my heart leaping, and a few days after that, I saw you walking toward me, so I pretended to be reading a book under a magnolia, then deliberately tore out a page and let you see me eat it.

My dad had told me ever since I was little that I shouldn't eat in front of anyone but my author, but I didn't hesitate for a second.

I thought back to when I first met Tohko.

Under a magnolia at the end of a long, long winter.

The weird girl with the braids from one grade up who puffed out her chest and made a vibrant declaration in the face of my bewilderment.

*"I am Tohko Amano in class eight of the second-years. As you can see, I am a book girl."*

It hadn't been by chance. Under that tree, her heart thrilling, Tohko had been listening for my footsteps.

Same with the way she'd made me write improv stories, and

made corrections to the pages with peculiar tastes that she brought to her lips through tears, and been at my side to encourage me constantly.

Tohko had been teaching me everything it took to become a writer as hard as she could.

I read the part where she said, *"You were so mean and stubborn; there were so many times you nearly discouraged me,"* and something hot welled up to fill my throat.

*"You've gotten good, Konoha."*

*"You've let me eat so many stories, Konoha."*

I told you the story about the ribbon at graduation, remember?
In second year, I made a wish on that ribbon.
That you would write me a novel someday.
I didn't manage to tie the ribbon up, but you picked up the ribbon I'd dropped and tied it around a branch for me.
I was so happy.
I suppose it was around then that my feelings for you started to transform inside me.
At first I thought I wanted you to write the novel my mom should have written.
But then I realized.
Your stories resembled my mom's, but there was something special, something decisive in the things you wrote, that wasn't in my mom's stories.
My mom's stories were like home cooking.
They were rustic and refreshing, but it was a flavor aimed at those closest to her and not something that could be aimed at masses of people.

The same way my dad told Aunt Kanako, "You're someone who needs to write." While I was partaking of the things you wrote every day, I had the same thought. You're someone who needs to write.

That the day would eventually come when I couldn't eat what you wrote.

Because it was a story that couldn't belong to me alone.

While I hoped that it would happen, I was very afraid of that day's arrival.

Because in my heart, I was always conflicted about not being able to tell you the truth.

Because I gradually began to be aware of you as a boy.

Because you look kind at first glance, but you're mean and cynical, and you're cowardly and a crybaby, and you're a troubled, high-maintenance kid.

And yet sometimes you'll do something so kind or docile that it makes my heart skip, and I think that's cowardice.

I can't be excitable. I have to look at you with jaded eyes because I have a mission to make you into a great author.

I became more and more conscious of you, to the point that I had to remind myself of those things, and my face would turn red or I would tell you, "Don't come near me!"

I even wavered, wondering if maybe I would be happier if I could spend my time with you the way things were, eating the snacks you wrote for me without thinking about making you into a writer.

And then I went to a fortune-teller I heard was accurate to talk to them.

She didn't mean—
When she'd stood outside a long time the day of the blizzard and caught a cold.

That fishy place that told her she'd been inside a zone of romantic slaughter since she was born, and about the scarf in summer, or the bear with a salmon in its mouth...

The upshot was, since I was in a zone of romantic slaughter, I should press ahead with other goals.

Why did she believe that fortune?! I'd been reading her letter so intently until then, and now, right here, all the power had gone out of it.

At the same time, the tears I'd pulled back once felt like they were going to slip out again with my lapse in focus.

This was, after all, the kind of person Tohko was.

She looked wise and elegant, but something was missing, and she hugged pillows shaking because she was afraid of ghosts, and tried to tie ribbons around the branches of trees because she believed in tricks to grant wishes, and knocked down mounds of books because she did a headstand in the clubroom, and was truly a menace to those around her and a hopeless president...But she always did her best—that—that was the kind of person she was.

That's why I sealed these feelings up and swore anew that I would make you into an author.
That from now on I would treat you as if I were your big sister.
Then the day you wrote a novel would be the day we parted.
But I stayed with you too long after all.
It's not good for me to be with you anymore.
I'm convinced that I would stop you from growing.
When you told me that you would never write a novel ever, I was flabbergasted. I thought I'd spoiled you and created a place you could escape to and closed off the path of writing, and it felt like my heart was cracking.

And yet whenever you cry, I can't help reaching out my hand again. I can't watch over you in silence as you suffer anymore. I feel your pain as if you're a part of me, and I do stupid things.

Sadness and pain are both important: people grow stronger by willing themselves to stand back up after they've fallen, and yet you thought you could stay the same unreliable Konoha forever, that you didn't have to write a novel.

That's not good.

Nanase got angry and called me selfish.

She came to see me the day of graduation and brought me your scarf.

She really is such a nice girl.

Nanase often consulted with me about you in the library. She was upset about how she got nervous whenever she saw you and ended up acting surly. Her straightforward feelings for you were so cute, they made me smile. I've always thought it would be nice if a girl like Nanase were your girlfriend.

I was jealous of her.

I still am.

I'm sure you and Nanase could walk side by side, helping each other.

I'm unnecessary.

Maybe I'm wrong, like Nanase said.

Maybe trying to pull away from you is an egotistical act.

Even now, Alissa's feelings aren't clear to me.

My dad told me to try reading Strait Is the Gate one day when I had someone I liked, and he gave me a copy.

I read it a ton of times after I met you, Konoha.

Why did Alissa leave Jerome even though she loved him?

Did she have to go alone?

Even though there was nothing standing in their way?

Each time I turned a page, I felt Alissa's pain and suffering as she tried to pull away, and it made my heart tremble.

Could Alissa have been wrong—?

However, Konoha.

I am a book girl who lives off stories as my nourishment, and I am Fumiharu Amano's daughter.

I cannot do something that might jeopardize the growth of an author.

Maybe my dad knew that Ryuto put poison into the coffee, and he let my mom drink it and then drank it himself anyway. Even now that doubt won't leave my heart.

Maybe the editor Fumiharu Amano sacrificed himself and his wife to become nourishment for the author Kanako Sakurai to write.

To let her write the supreme novel—

Like a transparent consommé with so many different ingredients blended together in it, even when my dad smiled with his clear eyes, you could never glimpse the deepest point in his heart. That's the kind of person he was.

So this is all just my "imagination," but...

While I fear something unforgivable, I wind up thinking that something like that might have happened. I am his daughter, after all, and I did inherit his blood.

My dad might have done something wrong, but I wanted to become someone who protected authors and made them grow, like my father.

I wanted to be your nourishment for writing, Konoha.

And when I think that Alissa might have gone through the narrow gate for Jerome's benefit, I feel like I can understand how she felt a little bit.

231

That even if she was wrong, the way Alissa felt, caring about Jerome, was true.

That for Alissa, it was "that which is superior."

I think that, and my heart grows lighter for just a moment. It grows pure and holy.

The two years I spent with you, Konoha, you were definitely my author alone.

You were the person more important to me than anything.

I'll never forget that.

I'll remember all the stories you wrote for me.

In my letters to Aunt Kanako, partway through it stops being my mom's words, and my own words start to mix in a lot.

I'm still confused about things, but I'm going to go through the narrow gate.

Please, Konoha, become an author who can shine a light on bleak truths, like you did for Aunt Kanako that day.

I don't have much left of Alt-Heidelberg, so instead I'll bring your scarf.

Good-bye.

I'll read your book somewhere under the same sky.

I clenched my jaw desperately and gulped back the tears that threatened to spill over.

I put the letter back in the envelope, stuck it inside *Strait Is the Gate*, put the book into my bag, and stood up.

When I turned out the light, the interior of the clubroom was wrapped in the cold darkness of night.

My throat almost tearing, my heart trembling, I thought fiercely.

I would go through the narrow gate, too.

I would move past it.

The wide road traveled with another was a much easier journey than the narrow road traveled alone.

If you were with someone else, you could grow strong, could support each other, wouldn't be lonely, could transform sadness into joy.

It was absolutely much nicer that way.

It was so many times more joyous than going alone.

But just as Tohko had gone alone, I, too, would go through the narrow gate and walk its narrow path alone.

The narrow gate isn't a gate for those who are chosen to go through. It's a gate that you find with your own eyes, steady yourself, and then walk through.

No matter how dark or cold or lonely or trying the road that leads from there might be, I had to become strong on my own and not with another.

Yes, I would become stronger.

I would steady myself.

I would go alone.

I would reach it alone.

Because I had grown full on the strength, the imagination, the stories for that from the book girl.

I went down the hall, descended the stairs, and went through the front entrance and out of the school building.

The warm golden backdrop had disappeared and there was no sign of a girl with braids. Only the dark night opened before me.

When I had walked my way alone through this night, I knew I could see her again.

After all, Tohko hadn't taken the scarf with her.

That was because she believed we would meet again.

\*       \*       \*

My love began at the time of our parting.

After becoming a third-year, I found out that the painting of Tohko was decorating the workroom in the music hall.

In the picture, Tohko has one of her braids undone, and she's wrapped in the golden light of sunset with a white lace curtain coiled around her naked body, next to a window, reading a book.

On her face is the smile like a violet that I always saw in that tiny room.

As if she were watching over me from there.

But for now, moving through the school yard at night toward the gate, I still didn't know about the painting.

I wasn't going to cry anymore.

From now on I would hide my sadness and smile like a mime.

Even if at times I was as famished as a spirit, at times made the decisions of a fool, was as covered in disgrace as a corrupted angel, I would hold the moon and flowers in my breast and continue walking like a wayfarer going to the holy land.

Then I would become a scribe who faced God.

An author who fixed their eyes on the truth, shone the light of imagination on it, and created a new world.

I went through the gate, then walked off in the opposite direction than Tohko had gone.

## Epilogue—Book Girl

Six years went by without seeing each other.

"Inoue!"

Kotobuki raised her hand to signal to me in the lobby of the airport. She was wearing a strawberry-pink short-sleeved sweater with a white skirt.

"Thanks for coming, Inoue."

"No problem. Looks like I'm late, though. Sorry."

"Are you busy with work?"

"I'm doing all right. Thanks for asking."

"Oh yeah? I've been seeing your books everywhere in magazine ads and bookstores."

I found myself unexpectedly captivated by her smile, which seemed to brighten the atmosphere. She'd been beautiful even in high school, but after going out into the world, it looked like she'd improved even further.

After graduating college, Kotobuki had started working at an office. She was taking a break for summer vacation today, going to Paris. To go see a performance by an opera singer who'd made a dramatic revival last year and was now widely talked about.

"It'd be great if you could see Omi, huh?"

"Yeah...but even if I can't talk to him, I'll be happy just being able to hear him sing," she murmured in a gentle voice. "I think Yuka would have enjoyed it, too."

Even now when Christmas came around, she still got a message from her best friend who'd passed away.

There was no question that he was the one sending them for Mito.

"I'll go see it, too, the next time they have a public performance."

"Thanks for coming all this way to see me off today."

She said this with a bright expression, then gazed at me mildly.

"...Do you remember...how I told you that I read *Strait Is the Gate* the day Tohko graduated? I meant it as a declaration that I would always love you. That Juliette married someone else for

236

Jerome and Alissa's sakes, but even if I wasn't your girlfriend anymore, I would still care about you. I went through 'the narrow gate' then, too."

A sunny smile spread over Kotobuki's face.

"I'm over it now, after all, but I'm glad that I kept caring for you."

"Thanks. You were too good for me as a girlfriend."

When I said that, she murmured shyly, "Don't be stupid," then waved and walked toward her departure gate.

I left the airport.

The sky was an almost blinding blue and the summer sun beat down on the asphalt.

As I headed to the station, it struck me anew that six years had gone by since that graduation ceremony.

After that day, Maki had safely given birth to a son. The boy, named Haruto, would be in elementary school next year. His face was like Ryuto's, but inside he was the exact duplicate of Maki, so Ryuto would lament that "He preaches to me and I can't stand it. He's such an uppity kid." Although Maki had come back sharply, "You do whatever you want and you don't work, so even your son worries about you."

Maki and Ryuto were both so fond of Haruto that it seemed he could do no wrong.

Maki got married three years ago.

When I found out who her husband was, I was floored.

He was the president of a trade company and he was *way* older than her. He had even been divorced and there were all sorts of nasty rumors about him. Everyone was even more against it and up in arms than when she'd given birth to Haruto.

But Maki's marriage happened right away. The daughter she had with him is three this year and her name is Hotaru. Of course, Maki gave this child her profound love, too.

Akutagawa took the civil servant exam and got a job with the government, and Miu got a job in the welfare field and spends her days interacting with children.

Ryuto was, as Maki said, suddenly going off on trips or getting part-time work at shady detective agencies, doing whatever he felt like.

Takeda had become a middle school teacher of all things. She made out with Ryuto so much that it embarrassed me.

Kanako won a literary prize in another country, and her reputation as an author had risen even further.

Her work titled *A Day for Yui* had been a sweetly kind—a sacred—story, the complete opposite of the things she'd written until then.

Occasionally I would hear about Tohko from Ryuto or Takeda.

How she'd graduated from college.

How her dissertation had been on Ogai Mori.

How she was working here.

But I never saw her once.

I went home to the apartment where I lived alone and booted up the computer in my study.

The day that Tohko had returned the manuscript I'd written for her and told me she couldn't eat it, I'd taken it and gone to see Mr. Sasaki.

That manuscript, with a parting scene added at the end and

finalized, was published as Miu Inoue's second book when I was a third-year in high school, and it became a best seller.

Just like with the first book, lots of people came to me about TV shows or a movie, but I turned them all down.

Because not just anyone could reproduce that smile like a violet, those clear eyes, that kind voice.

I wanted the people who read my book to picture their own book girl in their own hearts.

Requests for work come in without much interruption, although none of them are the explosive successes that my first book *Like the Open Sky* and my second book *Book Girl* were.

Ever since that day I decided to walk alone, I've kept writing.

"Konoha, your tea is ready."

I opened the door and Maika stuck her face in.

My little sister was in middle school now, and she would frequently come by my apartment because she wanted to help me out.

Apparently she thought it was fun to make meals and do laundry because Mom did everything for her at home.

Maika's possessions increased steadily at my apartment. Once summer break started, we were halfway living together, and I even had friends who teased, "Just get married already," so it was kind of a pain. I *told* 'em she was my little sister and everything.

The sweet aroma of lemon meringue pie wafted through the door.

"C'mon already, Konoha. Konoha—what are you doing?!"

Maika's eyes went wide.

I came out of my room wearing a white scarf around my neck.

"Why are you wearing a scarf? It's summertime!"

"Because it's summertime."

I went past Maika and onto the landing outside my front door.

When I stuck a stuffed bear wearing a Santa suit onto the wall beside the door with a thumbtack, Maika's eyes became even more shocked.

"What's with that bear? He's dressed like Santa and he's got a fish in his mouth! Did you draw this fish, Konoha? Why a Santa in the summer? Why a fish?"

"Does it look like a salmon?"

"A salmon?! Why does he have a salmon in his mouth? And why are you hanging it up right there? Is it some kind of good luck charm? Did you get stuck on a manuscript and go funny in the head?"

"What a mean thing to say. I'm on schedule."

"But if you hang up that bear and wear that scarf when the new manager is coming over, they'll think Miu Inoue is a weirdo."

"That's fine."

I smiled for her.

"Because the new editor is a *total* weirdo, too."

"Do you know them?"

"Yeah. You do, too."

"What?"

The Santa bear that Tohko had given me on Christmas Eve was looking at us, a salmon in his mouth.

I won't forget.

You've been in my heart all along.

The man of destiny is waiting for her, wearing a white scarf, in front of a bear with a salmon in its mouth.

She would come through that door any second.

The bell rang.

Maika ran to the room where the intercom was.

"See, now the manager's here! Take the bear down and take off that scarf quick! Inoue residence. Sorry to keep you waiting. Right. Okay. We've been expecting you. I'm unlocking it now."

The sound of the elevator climbing.

The sound of its doors opening to either side.

The sound of light footsteps approaching.

I closed my eyes and listened closely with a joyous feeling.

And then the bell rang, and I opened my eyes and turned the doorknob.

Hello, Mizuki Nomura here.

The Book Girl series has found its way to the conclusion.

The inspiration, in a continuation from the first volume, is Gide's *Strait Is the Gate*. Gide called this work a "recit" (or story) and he broke it into "romans" (or novels). I wanted to give some attention to this facet, but I wasn't able to touch on it in this volume.

Also, it would be correct to say that the "scribe" of the title is a "novelist," so since the author here includes the sense of "novelist," I went with "scribe." I hope you understand.

The diary I used in the story was utterly oppressive from the very first page. Gide left behind a huge number of letters and diaries, but I was shocked plenty of times and thought, *Should you really be writing about **that?!*** I couldn't tell how much was true, and as he toyed with my expectations, I got sucked in.

If he'd lived in modern times, I'm convinced he would keep a shocking diary of every detail on his blog.

I absolutely recommend those interested read it. It's the kind of thing that can change your values.

Now, at the very end, even unreliable Konoha was brave like a main character.

Tohko and Nanase each made their own decisions, too. Even if something painful happens, every kid can be happy. Because the thing that comes after the end is a beginning!

But for right now, I'm indulging in the lingering impression of an ending.

Thank you to everyone who's read this far.

When we met up, my manager would always bring me a fat stack of questionnaire postcards and reading them made me feel excited and embarrassed and all sorts of other things.

And a deep thank-you to those who wrote me letters and to those who talked about Book Girl on their websites. Every time I hear someone's beautiful thoughts, it encourages me.

At first, although I planned it out furiously, I was worried out of my mind about whether I could write these stories with my current skill level. As expected, every volume was an exercise in revision, revision, revision. All I can do is bow my head to my manager, who would engage me in long meetings every time.

It was this editor, too, who first gave me a push and said, "Let's write!" They brought everything they had to grappling with the series, and I believe *Book Girl* was a story I could only have written with this person.

I was also thrilled to always get such marvelous drawings from our illustrator, Miho Takeoka. I've been begging her to put out a *Book Girl* art book for the longest time, and it finally looks like it might happen! Once they decide when it's going to go on sale, I'll let you know!

The manga series has also started up. The artist is Rito Kohsaka. Tohko and Konoha look adorable in their kaleidoscope of expressions! The color is also translucent and gorgeous. It's on sale the twenty-second of even-numbered months from *GanGan Powered*. I hope you'll take a look!

There's one other thing I want to let you know about. I wrote a collaboration with *School Scarecase* in a collaborative short story collection that goes on sale in October. It also includes a collaboration I did with *Baka and Test: Summon the Beasts* that was published on the Internet. Plus it includes a collaboration on the Book Girl that Mr. Inoue of *Baka and Test* was gracious enough to write and sketches by Ms. Takeoka, so that makes it a must-see! I lobbied passionately for a _____ scene of Konoha, just so you know.

Next up is a Book Girl short story collection. I'd love to write some humorous stories or maybe some make-out stories. All that's left after that is side stories, but for those I'd want to write about "awesome, reliable Konoha." Argh, but it feels like so much effort to write again.

This volume came safely to its end, but I'd love it if we could talk a little longer and pretend it hadn't. I'll see you!

Mizuki Nomura<br>
July 7, 2008

# Afterword

When I hand over this drawing, my illustration work for this volume of BOOK GIRL will be at an end. All I've done is pray that I might be able to supply the drawings responsibly.

Thanks for all your hard work, Ms. Nomura! Thank you to the manager and designer who always dealt with us so untiringly.

I think everyone is waiting for us, happy and healthy, in the side stories, so I hope we'll see you there.

### Miho Takeoka

## Mizuki Nomura

Born in a tiny town in Fukushima, known to those who know it, she delighted in making up stories from a young age and dreamed of becoming a writer. She won the third Entame Award for outstanding new novel. Hobbies include morning naps, afternoon naps, evening naps, and sleeping in general.

## Miho Takeoka

Born July 1 in Tokyo, now a professional drawer of pictures living in Saitama. Her greatest loves are tea, rabbits, old books of illustrations, watercolor painting, and Gekkoso sketchbooks. She is happiest when drawing pictures or making something.

http://www.nezicaplant.com/ (Note that this website is in Japanese.)